SINDBAD THE SAILOR

AND OTHER TALES FROM THE ARABIAN NIGHTS

Some of the best-known children's stories are contained in *The Tales from the Arabian Nights* (also known as *The Thousand and One Nights*) which is a huge collection of tales passed down through the generations for over a thousand years. They were first introduced to the West at the beginning of the eighteenth century and since then there have been many different versions of the stories in print, pantomime and on film. Here are some of those stories retold directly from the authentic Arabic sources.

This collection includes the well-known tales of *Sindbad the Sailor* and *Ali Baba and the Forty Thieves*, as well as the lesser known *Tale of the Hunchback* and *The Barber of Baghdad*. The stories, which originate from Persia, India and Arabia, were the daily entertainment of everyday people. In this edition they are presented in a straightforward but not over-simplified way so that they are as fresh and exciting as they were when they were first told.

N. J. Dawood was born in Baghdad and came to England in 1945 as an Iraq State Scholar. He is best known for his translation of *The Koran*, which was first published as a Penguin Classic in 1956, and has since been reprinted thirty-three times. In 1959 he founded The Arabic Advertising and Publishing Co. Ltd, London, which is now one of the major producers of Arabic translations and typesetting outside the Middle East.

The illustrations are from the famous original engravings on wood made by William Harvey in 1839.

Retold from the original Arabic by

N. J. DAWOOD

Sindbad the Sailor
and Other Tales from
The Arabian Nights

Engravings on wood from original designs by
WILLIAM HARVEY

PUFFIN BOOKS

This version follows Macnaghten's Calcutta edition of *The Thousand and One Nights* (1839–42) but the first Bulaq edition (1835) has been consulted wherever the Macnaghten text appeared faulty.

PUFFIN BOOKS

Published by the Penguin Group
Penguin Books Ltd, 27 Wrights Lane, London W8 5TZ, England
Penguin Books USA Inc., 375 Hudson Street, New York, New York 10014, USA
Penguin Books Australia Ltd, Ringwood, Victoria, Australia
Penguin Books Canada Ltd, 10 Alcorn Avenue, Toronto, Ontario, Canada M4V 3B2
Penguin Books (NZ) Ltd, 182–190 Wairau Road, Auckland 10, New Zealand

Penguin Books Ltd, Registered Offices: Harmondsworth, Middlesex, England

This edition first published in the USA by Doubleday & Company, Inc. 1978
Published in Puffin Books 1989
Reissued in this edition 1994
3 5 7 9 10 8 6 4

Filmset by Datix International Limited, Bungay, Suffolk
Printed in England by Clays Ltd, St Ives plc
Set in 12/15 pt Monophoto Plantin

To Juliet, Richard, Norman,
and Andrew

Contents

PROLOGUE

THE TALE OF KING SHAHRIYAR AND HIS BROTHER, SHAHZAMAN

Once upon a time, there ruled over India and China a mighty king, who commanded great armies and had numerous courtiers, followers, and servants. He left two sons, both famed for their horsemanship – especially the older, who inherited his father's kingdom and governed it with such justice that all his subjects loved him. He was called King Shahriyar. His brother was named Shahzaman and was King of Samarkand.

The two brothers continued to reign happily in their kingdoms, and after twenty years King Shahriyar longed to see Shahzaman. He ordered his vizier to go to Samarkand and invite Shahzaman to his court.

The vizier set out promptly on his errand and journeyed many days and nights through deserts and wildernesses until he arrived in Shahzaman's city and was admitted to his presence. He gave him King Shahriyar's greetings and told him of his master's wish to see him. King Shahzaman was overjoyed at the thought of visiting his brother. He made ready to leave his kingdom, and sent out his tents, camels, mules, servants, and retainers. Then he appointed his vizier as his deputy and set out for his brother's dominions.

At midnight, however, he suddenly remembered a present which he wished to give his brother but which he had left at the palace. He returned alone to fetch it. Entering his private chamber, he was outraged to find his beautiful queen, whose affection he had never doubted, entertaining a palace slave.

'If this can happen when I am scarcely out of my city,' he thought, 'what will this wicked woman do when I am far away?'

He drew his sword and slew them both. Then he rejoined his courtiers and journeyed on until he reached his brother's capital.

Shahriyar rejoiced at his coming. He went out to meet Shahzaman, took him in his arms, and welcomed him affectionately. But as they sat chatting, he noticed that Shahzaman, who was brooding over his wife's disloyalty, looked pale and sullen. Shahriyar said nothing about this, thinking that his brother might be worrying over the affairs of the kingdom he had left behind. Day after day Shahriyar tried to distract him, but all to no avail. At last he invited him to go hunting, hoping that the sport might cheer his spirits, but Shahzaman refused, and Shahriyar had to go to the hunt alone.

Meanwhile, Shahzaman sat at a window overlooking the royal garden, and saw one of the palace doors open and twenty women and twenty slaves appear. In their midst was his brother's Queen, a woman of rare beauty. They made their way to the fountain and sat down on the grass, each slave choosing a woman for his companion. Then the King's wife called out, 'Come, Masood!' and a slave at once ran up to her and sat down beside her. There they all remained, feasting together, till nightfall.

'By Allah,' said Shahzaman to himself, 'my misfortune was nothing beside this.'

He was no longer unhappy, but ate and drank, being hungry after his long abstinence.

When Shahriyar returned from the hunt he was surprised to see his brother restored to health and good spirits.

'How is it, brother,' he asked, 'that when I last saw you, you were so pale and sad, and now you look well and contented?'

'As for my sadness,' Shahzaman replied, 'I will now tell you the reason. Know that after I had received your invitation I made preparations for the journey and set out from my capital; but I had forgotten the pearl that was my present for you, and went back to the palace for it. There in my room I found my wife in the company of a slave. I killed them both. Then I came on to your kingdom, though my mind was troubled with unhappy thoughts.'

When he heard this, Shahriyar was curious to know the rest of the story, upon which Shahzaman related to him all that he had seen that day from the window.

'I will not believe it,' Shahriyar exclaimed, 'unless I see it with my own eyes!'

'Then let it be known that you intend to hunt again,' suggested his brother. 'But hide with me here, and you will see what I saw.'

And so King Shahriyar announced his intention to set out on another expedition. Soldiers, with their tents, left the city, and Shahriyar followed them. As soon as they had encamped, he gave orders to his slaves that no one was to be admitted to the King's tent. Then, disguising himself, he returned unnoticed to the palace, where his brother was waiting for him. They sat together at one of the windows overlooking the garden. It was not long before the Queen and her women appeared with the slaves and thus King Shahriyar saw that what his brother had told him was true.

Crazed with anger, he put his Queen to death, together with all her women and the slaves. And after that he made it his custom to marry a young girl every day and kill her the next morning. This he continued to do for three years, until an outcry arose among the people, and some of them left the country with their daughters.

At last a day came when the King's vizier searched the city in vain for a wife for his master. Finding none, and dreading the King's anger, he returned home with a heavy heart.

Now, the vizier himself had two daughters. The older was called Shahrazad, and the younger Dunyazad. Shahrazad was both beautiful and accomplished: she knew the works of poets and the legends of ancient kings.

Shahrazad noticed her father's anxiety and asked what made him so sad. The vizier told her the reason. 'Dear Father,' she said, 'give me in marriage to the King. Either I will die a martyr's death, or I will live and save my countrymen's daughters.'

Her proposal filled the vizier with horror. He warned her how dangerous it would be; but she had made up her mind and would not listen to his advice.

So the vizier arrayed his daughter in bridal garments, decked her with jewels, and made ready to announce her wedding to the King.

When she said good-by to her sister, Shahrazad gave her these instructions: 'After I have been received by the King I shall send for you. When you come, you must say, 'Tell us, sister, some tale of marvel to pass the night.' Then I will tell you a tale which, if Allah wills, shall be the means of our deliverance.'

So the vizier went with his daughter to the King. And when the King had taken Shahrazad to his chamber she wept and said, 'I have a young sister to whom I dearly wish to say a last farewell.'

The King sent for Dunyazad, who came and threw her arms around her sister's neck and sat down beside her.

Then Dunyazad said to Shahrazad, 'Tell us, sister, a tale of marvel so that the night may pass pleasantly.'

'Gladly,' she answered, 'if the King permits me.'

The King, who was troubled with sleeplessness, gave her leave and eagerly listened to Shahrazad's story:

SINDBAD THE SAILOR AND SINDBAD
THE PORTER

Once upon a time, in the reign of the Caliph
Harun al-Rashid, there lived in Baghdad a poor
man who earned his living by carrying loads upon
his head. He was called Sindbad the Porter.

One day, as he was staggering under a heavy
load in the heat of the summer sun, he passed a
merchant's house that stood in a pleasant, shaded
spot on the roadside. The ground around it was
well swept and watered, and, seeing a broad
wooden bench just outside the gates, Sindbad put
down his load and sat there to rest and to wipe
away the sweat that trickled down his forehead. A

cool, fresh breeze blew through the doorway, and from within came the melodious strains of a lute and singing voices. They mingled with the songs of pigeons and thrushes, larks and turtledoves.

Filled with great joy, he went up to the open door and saw a courtyard with a beautiful garden, around which stood numerous slaves and servants, and such a crowd of attendants as can be found only in the courts of mighty kings. And all about the place hung the aroma of the choicest meats and wines.

Still marveling at the splendor of the palace, Sindbad lifted up his burden and was about to go on his way when a handsome and well-dressed little page came to him and took him by the hand, saying, 'Please come in; my master wishes to speak with you.'

The porter refused very politely, but the boy pressed him to go in. So Sindbad left his load with the doorkeeper and followed the page into the house.

He was led into a magnificent hall, where a distinguished company of nobles was seated according to rank. Before the nobles were tables spread with the richest meats and wines and gaily decked with flowers and fruit. On one side of the hall sat beautiful slave girls who sang and made music; and on the other sat the host, a venerable old man with a long white beard. Bewildered by what he saw, the porter thought to himself, 'This must be either a corner of paradise or the palace of some king.'

He greeted them all politely, kissed the ground before them, and wished them joy, then stood in silence.

The master of the house welcomed him kindly and asked him to sit down. Then he ordered his slaves to set before him a choice of delicate foods and pressed him to eat. Sindbad pronounced a blessing on the food and fell to. When he had eaten his fill he washed his hands and thanked the old sheikh for his hospitality.

'You are welcome, my friend,' said the host, 'and may this day bring you joy. We would gladly know your name and calling.'

'My name is Sindbad,' he answered, 'by trade a porter.'

'How strange a chance!' said the old man, smiling. 'My name, too, is Sindbad. They call me Sindbad the Sailor, and people marvel at my strange history. I will now tell you the story of my seven voyages, and of the hardships I suffered before I rose to my present state and became the lord of this mansion where we are now assembled.'

THE FIRST VOYAGE
OF SINDBAD THE SAILOR

Know, my friends, that my father was the chief merchant of this city and one of its richest men. He died while I was still a child, leaving me great wealth and many estates and farmlands. As soon as I came to manhood and had control of my inheritance, I took to extravagant living. I wore the most expensive clothes, ate and drank lavishly, and went about with wasteful young men, thinking that this mode of life would last for ever.

It was not long before I woke up to my folly only to find that I had squandered my entire fortune. This made me stop and think, for I did not much like the idea of being poor. So I sold what remained of my lands and household goods and made up my mind to trade with the proceeds in foreign countries.

I bought a large quantity of merchandise and prepared for a long voyage. Then I joined a company of merchants and set sail in a river ship bound for the port of Basra. There we put to sea and voyaged many days and nights from isle to isle and from shore to shore, buying and selling and exchanging goods wherever the ship anchored. At last we came to a little island as beautiful as the garden of Eden. Here the captain of our ship cast anchor and put out the landing planks.

The passengers went ashore and started to light a fire. Some busied themselves with cooking and washing, some fell to eating and drinking and making merry, while others, like myself, set out to explore the island. While we were thus occupied we suddenly heard the captain cry out to us from the ship, 'All aboard, quickly! Abandon everything and run for your lives! The mercy of Allah be upon you, for this is no island but a gigantic whale floating on the bosom of the sea, on whose back the sands have settled and trees have grown since the world was young! When you lit the fire the whale felt the heat and moved. Hurry, I say, or soon it will plunge into the sea and you will all be lost!'

Hearing the captain's cries, the passengers made for the ship in panic-stricken flight, leaving behind their cooking pots and other belongings. Some reached the ship in safety, but others did not, for suddenly the island shook beneath our feet and dived with all that stood upon it to the bottom of the ocean.

Together with my luckless companions, I was swallowed up by the tide, but Providence came to my aid, casting in my way a large wooden trough that had been used by the ship's company for washing. I held fast to the trough and paddled away with my feet as the waves tossed and buffeted me on every side. Meanwhile the captain hoisted sail and set off with the other passengers. I followed the ship with my eyes until it vanished from sight, and resigned myself to certain death.

Darkness soon closed in upon the ocean. All that night and throughout the following day I drifted on, lashed by the wind and the waves, until the trough brought me to the steep shores of a densely wooded island, where trees hung over the sea.

I caught hold of one of the branches and used it to scramble ashore. Arriving on dry land, after fighting so long for my life, I found that I had lost the use of my legs, and my feet began to smart from the bites of fish.

Tired and aching all over, I sank into a deathlike sleep, and it was not until the next morning when the sun rose that I came to my senses. But my feet were so sore and swollen that I could move about only by crawling on my knees. By good fortune, the island had many fruit trees, which provided me with food, and springs of fresh water, so that after a few days my body was restored to strength and my spirits revived. I cut myself a stick from the branch of a tree, and with the help of it set out to explore the island and to admire the fine plants that grew there.

One day, while roaming over the beach in an unfamiliar part of the island, I caught sight of a strange object in the distance that appeared to be some wild beast or sea monster. Drawing near and looking at it more closely, I saw that it was a noble mare of uncommonly high stature, tied to a tree. On seeing me, the mare gave an ear-splitting neigh that made me take to my heels in terror. Presently there emerged from under the ground a man, who pursued me, shouting, 'Who are you and where have you come from? What are you doing here?'

'Sir,' I replied, 'I am a luckless voyager, abandoned in the middle of the sea; but it was Allah's will that I should be rescued from the fury of the waves and cast upon this island.'

The stranger took me by the hand and led me to an underground cave, where he placed some food before me and invited me to eat. He then asked about the fortunes of my voyage, and I related to him all that had befallen me.

'Now, what brings *you* here?' I asked my host.

'I am one of the many grooms of King Mahrajan,' he replied. 'We have charge of all his horses, and every month we bring them to pasture in this meadow. This evening, when we have finished our work, I will take you to our King and show you our city. Allah be praised for this happy meeting; for had you not chanced to cross our path you would have surely died in the solitude of these wild parts.'

I thanked him and called down blessings upon him. We went out of the cave into the open, and while we were talking, the other grooms, each leading a horse, approached us. My companion explained to them how I had come to be there, and after exchanging greetings we rode to the city of King Mahrajan.

As soon as the King was informed of my arrival he summoned me to his presence. He marveled at my story, saying, 'By Allah, my son, your escape was a miracle.'

I rose rapidly in the King's favor and soon became a trusted courtier. He vested me with robes of honor and appointed me Registrar of Shipping at the port of his kingdom. During my stay I saw many marvels and met travelers from different foreign lands. One day I entered the King's throne room and found him entertaining a company of Indians. I exchanged greetings with them and asked them about their country.

In the course of the conversation I learned that there were several castes in India. The noblest of them were skilled breeders of horses and cattle and were known for their piety and fair dealing.

Not far from the King's dominions there is a desert island where at night is heard a mysterious beating of drums and rattle of tambourines. It was there that I once saw a fish two hundred cubits in length, and another with a head resembling an owl's. This I saw with my own eyes, and many other things no less strange and wondrous.

Whenever I walked along the quay I talked with the sailors and travelers from far countries, asking whether any of them had heard tell of the city of Baghdad and how far off it lay, for I never lost hope that I would one day find my way back to my native land. But there was none who knew of that city, and as the days passed away my longing for home weighed heavily on my heart.

One day, however, as I stood on the wharf, leaning on my stick and gazing out to sea, a ship bearing a large company of merchants came sailing into the harbor. As soon as it was moored, the sails were furled and landing planks put out. The crew began to unload the cargo, and I stood by, entering up the merchandise in my register. When they had finished I asked the captain if all the goods had now been brought ashore.

'Sir,' he replied, 'in the ship's hold I still have a few bales that belonged to a merchant who was drowned at an early stage of our voyage. We will put them up for sale and take the money to his people in Baghdad, the City of Peace.'

'What was the merchant's name?' I asked.

'Sindbad,' he answered.

I looked more closely into his face and, recognizing him at once, uttered a joyful cry.

'Why, these goods are mine!' I exclaimed. 'I am Sindbad, who was left to drown with many others when the great whale plunged into the sea. But the waves cast me onto the shore of this island. I tell you I am the true owner of these goods, which are my only possessions in the world.'

The captain now recognized me. He marveled at my story and was overjoyed to see me alive. My goods were brought ashore, and I found the bales intact and sealed as I had left them. I selected some of the choicest and most precious articles as presents for King Mahrajan, and had them carried by the sailors to the royal palace, where I laid them at his feet. I told the King of the sudden arrival of my ship and the recovery of all my goods. He was astonished at this chance, and in return for my presents bestowed upon me priceless treasures.

I sold my wares at a substantial profit and re-equipped myself with the finest produce of that island. When all was ready for the homeward voyage, I presented myself at the King's court and thanked him for the many favors he had shown me, and he gave me leave to return to my land and people.

Then we set sail, and after voyaging for many days and nights arrived safely in Basra. I spent only a few days in that town and then, loaded with treasure, set out for Baghdad. I was overjoyed to be back in my native city and, hastening to my old street, entered my own house, where, by and by, my friends and kinsmen came to greet me.

I bought fine houses and rich farmlands, serving girls and African slaves, and became richer than I had ever been before. I kept open house for my old companions and, soon forgetting the hardships of my voyage, resumed my former mode of living.

That is the story of the first of my adventures. Tomorrow, if Allah wills, I will relate to you the tale of my second voyage.

The day was drawing to its close, and Sindbad the Sailor invited Sindbad the Porter to join the guests in the evening meal. When the feast was finished he gave him a hundred pieces of gold, saying, 'You have delighted us with your company today.'

The porter thanked him for his generous gift and departed, marveling at all he had heard.

Next morning he went again to the house of the old sheikh, who received him courteously and seated him by his side. Presently the other guests arrived, and when they had feasted and made merry, Sindbad the Sailor began:

THE SECOND VOYAGE
OF SINDBAD THE SAILOR

For some time after my return from my first voyage I continued to lead a free and easy life, but I soon longed to travel again about the world and to visit distant cities and islands in quest of profit and adventure. So I bought a great quantity of goods, made preparations for a new voyage, and sailed down the river Tigris to Basra. There I joined a band of merchants and embarked in a fine vessel that set sail the same day.

Helped by a favorable wind, we voyaged for many days from port to port and from island to island; and wherever we cast anchor we sold and bartered our goods, and haggled with officials and merchants. At last our ship reached the shores of an uninhabited island, rich in fruit and flowers, and echoing with the singing of birds and the murmur of crystal streams.

Here passengers and crew went ashore, and we all set off to enjoy the delights of the island. I strolled through the green meadows, leaving my companions far behind, and sat down in a shady thicket to eat a simple meal by a spring. Lulled by the soft and fragrant breeze that blew around me, I lay upon the grass and presently fell asleep.

I cannot tell how long I slept, but when I woke I saw none of my companions and feared the ship had left. I ran in frantic haste toward the sea, and on reaching the shore saw the vessel, a white speck upon the vast blue ocean, dissolving into the far horizon.

Broken with terror and despair, I threw myself upon the sand, crying, 'Now your end has come, Sindbad! The jar that drops a second time is sure to break!' I repented my folly in venturing again upon the perils of the sea, and wished with all my heart that I had stayed safe at home. I wandered about aimlessly for some time, and then climbed into a tall tree. From the top I gazed in all directions, but could see nothing except the sky, the trees, the birds, the sands, and the boundless ocean. As I scanned the interior of the island more closely, however, I gradually became aware of a white object looming in the distance. At once

I climbed down the tree and made my way toward it. Drawing near, I found to my astonishment it was a white dome of extraordinary size. Walking all around it, I could see no door or entrance of any kind; and so smooth and slippery was its surface that any attempt to climb it would have been fruitless. I made a mark in the sand near its base, walked around it again, and found that its circumference measured more than fifty paces.

While I was doing this, the sun was suddenly hidden from my view as by a great cloud and the world grew dark around me. I lifted up my eyes toward the sky and was confounded to see a gigantic bird with enormous wings, which, as it flew through the air, screened the sun, hiding it from the island.

This strange sight instantly brought back to my mind a story I had heard in my youth from pilgrims and adventurers: how in a far island dwelt a bird of monstrous size called the roc, which fed its young on elephants; and at once I realized that the white dome was none other than a roc's egg. In a twinkling, the bird alighted upon the egg, covered it completely with its wings, and stretched out its legs behind it on the ground. And in this posture it went to sleep.

Rising swiftly, I unwound my turban from my head, then doubled it and twisted it into a rope with which I tied myself securely to one of the great talons of the monster.

'It may be,' I said to myself, 'that this bird will

carry me away to a civilized land; wherever I am set down, it will surely be better than an uninhabited island.'

I lay awake all night, fearing to close my eyes lest the bird should fly away with me while I slept. At daybreak the roc rose from the egg and, spreading its wings, took to the air with a terrible cry. I clung fast to its talon as it winged its flight through the void and soared higher and higher until it almost touched the sky. After some time it began to drop and, floating swiftly downward, came to earth on the brow of a steep hill.

In great fear I hastened to untie my turban before the roc became aware of my presence. Scarcely had I released myself when the monster darted off toward a great black object lying near, clutched it in its claws, and took wing again. As it rose in the air I saw that this was a serpent of immeasurable length and with its prey the bird vanished from sight.

Now to find out where I was! I was looking out over an exceedingly deep and wide valley. On all sides there were rocky mountains whose towering summits no man could ever climb. I was stricken with fear and repented my rashness.

'If only I had stayed on that island!' I thought to myself. 'There at least I lacked neither fruit nor water, while these barren rocks offer nothing to eat or drink. I have indeed come into worse misfortune.'

On making my way down the hill I marveled to

see that the ground was thickly covered with the rarest diamonds, so that the entire valley was bathed in a glorious light. But crawling among the glittering stones were deadly snakes and vipers, dread keepers of the fabulous treasure. Thicker and longer than giant palm trees, they could have swallowed whole elephants at one gulp. They were returning to their sunless dens, for by day they hid themselves from their enemies the rocs and the eagles, and moved about only at night.

Half crazed with terror, I roamed the valley all day searching for a shelter where I might pass the night. At dusk I crawled into a narrow-mouthed cave and blocked its entrance with a great stone. At daybreak I rolled back the stone and went out of my hiding place.

As I walked about I noticed a great piece of flesh come tumbling down into the valley from rock to rock. On examining it, I found it to be a whole sheep, skinned and drawn. I was deeply puzzled by the mystery, for there was not a soul in sight; but at that moment there flashed across my mind the memory of a story I had once heard from travelers who had visited the Diamond Mountains – how men obtained the diamonds from this remote and treacherous valley by a strange device. Before sunrise they would throw whole carcasses of sheep from the top of the mountains, so that the gems on which they fell cut through the soft flesh and became embedded in it. At midday rocs and mighty vultures would swoop down upon the mutton and carry it away in their talons toward their nests in the mountain heights. Shouting loudly, the merchants would then rush at the birds and force them to drop the meat and fly away, after which all that remained was for them to look through the carcasses and pick out the diamonds.

As I recalled this story, a plan of escape formed in my mind. I selected a great quantity of substantial stones and hid them about me; I filled my pockets with them and pressed them into the folds of my belt and garments. Then I unrolled my turban, stuffed it with more diamonds, twisted it into a rope as I had done before and, lying under the carcass, tied it firmly to my chest. I had not remained long in that position when I suddenly felt myself lifted from the ground by a huge vulture whose talons had tightly closed upon the meat. The bird climbed higher and higher and finally alighted upon a mountaintop. As soon as it began to tear at the flesh there arose from the nearby rocks a hue and cry, at which the bird took fright and flew away. At once I freed myself and sprang to my feet.

A man came running to the spot and stopped in alarm as he saw me. Without uttering a word, he cautiously bent over the carcass to examine it, looking at me suspiciously all the while, but, finding no diamonds, he wrung his hands and started back in fear.

'Who are you?' he cried. 'And what are you doing here?'

'Do not be alarmed, sir,' I replied. 'I am no thief but an honest man, a merchant by profession. My story is very strange, and the adventure that has brought me to these mountains is more extraordinary than all the marvels men have seen or heard. But first, please accept some of these diamonds, which I myself gathered in the fearful valley below.'

I took some splendid jewels from my pocket and offered them to him, saying, 'These will bring you all the riches you can desire.'

The merchant was overjoyed at the unexpected gift; he thanked me warmly and called down blessings upon me. While we were talking, several other merchants came up from the mountainside. They crowded around us and listened in amazement to my story. Then they led me to their tent. They gave me food and drink, and I slept soundly for many hours. Early next day, we set out from our tent and, journeying over a vast range of mountains, came at last to the seashore. After a short voyage we arrived at a pleasant, densely wooded island, covered with trees so huge that beneath only one of them a hundred men could shelter from the sun.

There I saw a gigantic beast called the karkadan, or rhinoceros, which grazes in the fields like a cow or buffalo. It is as big as a camel and has a single horn in the middle of its forehead. The rhinoceros attacks the elephant, impales it upon its horn, and carries it aloft from place to place until its victim dies. Before long, however, the elephant's fat melts in the heat of the sun and, dripping down into the rhinoceros' eyes, blinds it, so that the beast blunders helplessly along and finally drops dead. Then the roc swoops down upon both animals and carries them off to its nest in the high mountains. I also saw many strange breeds in that island.

I sold several of my diamonds for a large sum and exchanged more for a vast quantity of merchandise. Then we set sail and traded from port to port and from island to island, at last arriving safely in Basra. After a few days I set out for Baghdad, the City of Peace.

Loaded with precious goods and the finest of my diamonds, I hastened to my old street and entered my own house, rejoicing to see my friends and kinsfolk. I gave them gold and presents, and distributed a large sum among the poor of the city.

Soon I forgot the perils and hardships of my travels, and took again to extravagant living. I ate well, dressed well, and kept open house for innumerable gallants and merry companions.

From far and near, men came to hear me speak of my adventures and to learn from me the news of foreign lands. All were astounded at the dangers I had escaped and wished me joy of my return. Such was my second voyage.

Tomorrow, my friends, if Allah wills, I shall

relate to you the extraordinary tale of my third voyage.

The famous mariner stopped speaking, and the guests marveled at his story.

When the evening feast was over, Sindbad the Sailor gave Sindbad the Porter a hundred pieces of gold, which he took with thanks and blessings, and departed, lost in wonderment at all he had heard.

Next day the porter rose and, after reciting his morning prayers, went to the house of his illustrious friend, who received him kindly and seated him by his side. And when all the guests were gathered, Sindbad the Sailor began:

The Third Voyage
of Sindbad the Sailor

Know, my friends, that for some years after my return to Baghdad my life was happy and tranquil. But I grew weary of my idleness and once again longed to roam the world in search of fresh adventures. Forgetting all I had been through, I resolved to set out on another voyage. I bought some more goods, took them down the river Tigris, and set sail from Basra with a band of honest merchants.

We called at many foreign ports and traded profitably with our merchandise. One day, however, while we were sailing in mid-ocean, we heard the captain of our ship, who was on deck scanning the horizon, suddenly break into a loud lament. He beat himself about the face, tore at his beard, and rent his clothes.

'We are lost!' he cried, as we crowded around him. 'The treacherous wind has driven us off our course toward that island which you see before you. It is the Isle of Zughb, where dwell a race of dwarfs more akin to apes than men. No voyager has ever escaped alive from their clutches!'

Scarcely had he uttered these words than a multitude of apelike savages appeared on the beach and swam toward the ship. In a few moments they were upon us, thick as a swarm of locusts. Barely two feet in height, they were the ugliest of living creatures, with gleaming yellow eyes and bodies thickly covered with black fur. And so numerous were they that we did not dare to fight them or try to drive them away, lest they should set upon us and kill us to a man by force of numbers.

They scrambled up the masts, gnawed the cables with their teeth, and bit them to shreds. Then they seized the helm and steered the vessel to their island. When the ship had run ashore, the dwarfs carried us one by one to the beach and, promptly pushing off again, climbed on board and sailed away.

We set out to search for food and water and by good fortune came upon some fruit trees and a running stream. Here we refreshed ourselves, and then wandered about the island until at length we sighted among the trees a massive building, where we hoped to pass the night in safety. Drawing near, we found that it was a towering palace surrounded by a high wall, with a great ebony door, which stood open. We entered the spacious courtyard, but saw no one there. In one corner lay a great heap of bones, and on the far side were a broad bench, an open oven, pots and pans of enormous size, and many iron spits for roasting.

Exhausted and sick at heart, we lay down in the courtyard and went to sleep. At sunset we were awakened by a noise like thunder. The earth shook beneath our feet and we saw a colossal black giant approaching from the doorway. He was a fearsome sight – tall as a palm tree, with red eyes burning in his head like coals of fire; his mouth was a dark well, with lips that drooped, like a camel's, loosely over his chest, while his ears, like a pair of large round disks, hung back over his shoulders; his fangs were as long as the tusks of a boar, and his nails were like the claws of a lion.

The sight of this monster struck terror into our hearts, we cowered motionless on the ground as we watched him stride across the yard and sit down on the bench. For a few moments he looked at us one by one in silence; then he got up, reached out toward me, lifted me up by the neck, and began feeling my body as a butcher would a lamb. Finding me little more than skin and bone, he flung me to the ground and, picking up each of my companions in turn, pinched and prodded them and set them down until at last he came to the captain.

Now, the captain was a well-built fellow, tall and broad-shouldered. The giant gripped him as a butcher grips a fatted ram, thrust an iron spit through him, and, lighting the fire in the oven, carefully turned him around and around before it until he was well cooked, and then ate him. After he had finished his meal, the ogre went to sleep on the bench and his snores were as loud as the grunts of a wild bull. When morning came, he rose and went out of the palace, leaving us half crazed with terror.

As soon as we were certain that the monster had gone, we began lamenting our evil fortune and wished we had been drowned in the sea or killed by the apes. We left the palace to search for some hiding place, but could find no shelter in any part of the island and had no choice but to return to the palace in the evening. Night came, and with it the black giant, announcing his approach with a noise like thunder. He snatched up one of the merchants and prepared his supper as on the night before; then, stretching himself out to sleep, he snored the night away.

Next morning, when the giant had gone, we discussed our desperate plight.

'By Allah,' cried one of the merchants, 'let us rather throw ourselves into the sea than remain alive to be roasted and eaten!'

'Listen, my friends,' said another, 'we must kill this monster, for only by destroying him can we end his wickedness and save good men from his cruelty.'

These words were received with general approval: so I got up in turn and addressed the company.

'If we are all agreed to kill this monster,' I said, 'let us first build a raft on which we can escape if our plot miscarries. Maybe our raft will take us to some other island, where we can board a ship bound for our country. If we are drowned, we shall at least escape roasting and die a martyr's death.'

'By Allah,' cried the others, 'that is a wise plan.'

So we set to work at once. We hauled several logs from the great pile of wood stacked beside the oven, and carried them out of the palace. Then we fastened them together into a raft, which we left ready on the seashore.

In the evening, the earth shook beneath us as the black giant burst into the yard, barking and snarling like a mad dog. Once more he seized upon the stoutest of my companions and prepared his meal. When he had eaten his fill, he lay down on the bench, as was his custom, and went to sleep.

Noiselessly we now rose, took two of the great iron spits from the oven, and thrust them into the fire. As soon as they were red-hot we carried them over to the snoring monster and plunged their ends into his eyes. He gave a deafening shriek that cast us back onto the ground many yards away. Then he leaped up from the bench and groped for us with outstretched hands, but, as he could not see where we were, we managed to get out of the palace and made off toward the beach. As soon as we reached the water we launched our raft and jumped on board; but scarcely had we rowed a few yards when we saw the blind savage running toward us, guided by a female of his own kind. On reaching the shore they stood howling at us for a while, and then caught up massive boulders and hurled them at our raft with stupendous force. Missile followed missile until all but two of my companions were drowned; but we three who escaped soon managed to paddle beyond the range of the flying boulders.

Lashed by the waves, we drifted on in the open sea for a whole day and a whole night until we were cast upon the shore of another island. Half dead with hunger and exhaustion, we threw ourselves upon the sand and fell asleep.

On awaking next morning, we found ourselves encircled by a great serpent, which lay about us in a coil. Before we could move a limb the beast suddenly lifted its head, seized one of my companions, and swallowed him. Presently, however, the serpent glided away, leaving us two stricken with grief at the horrible fate of our comrade and amazed at our own narrow escape.

'By Allah,' we cried, 'we have fled from one

form of death only to meet with another equally hideous. How shall we escape this serpent? There is no strength or help except in Allah!'

The warmth of the newborn day gave us fresh courage, and we struck inland to search for food and water. Before nightfall we climbed into a tall tree and perched ourselves as best we could upon the topmost branches. But as soon as darkness fell we heard a fearful hissing and a noise of heavy movement on the ground; and in a twinkling the serpent had seized my friend and carried him off. That was the end of the last of my companions.

At daybreak I climbed down from my hiding place. My first thought was to throw myself into the sea and thus end a life that had already endured more than its share of hardships and ordeals. But when I reached the shore my courage failed me, for life is very precious. I clung instinctively to the hope of a speedy rescue, and a plan to protect myself from the serpent began to form in my mind.

I collected some thick planks of wood and fastened them together into a coffin-shaped box, complete with lid. When evening came I shut myself in, shielded on all sides by strong boards. By and by the snake approached and circled around me, writhing and squirming. All night long its dreadful hissing sounded in my ears, but with the approach of morning it turned away and vanished into the undergrowth.

When the sun rose, I left my shelter and made for the shore. What should I now see but a ship sailing near the island!

At once I tore off a great branch from a tree and, yelling at the top of my voice, waved it frantically above my head. The crew must have seen my signal, for to my great joy the ship suddenly turned off its course and headed for the island.

When I came aboard, the captain gave me a clean robe to put on and offered me food and drink. Little by little I regained my strength, and after a few days of rest became my old self again. I rendered thanks to God for rescuing me from my ordeal, and soon my past sufferings were no more than half-forgotten dreams.

After a few days we cast anchor at a small island. On board our ship were some merchants, who now went ashore with their goods to trade with the people. While I was standing idly by, watching the busy scene, the captain came up and spoke to me.

'Listen, my friend,' he said, 'you say you are a penniless stranger who has lost everything at sea. I will make you an offer that will be greatly to your advantage. A few years ago I carried in my ship a merchant who, alas, was left behind on a desert island. No news has since been heard of him, and no one knows whether he is alive or dead. Take his goods and trade with them, and a share of the profit shall be yours. The remainder of the money I will take back to the merchant's family in Baghdad.'

I thanked the captain with all my heart. He ordered the crew to unload the merchandise and called the ship's clerk to enter up the bales in his register.

'Whose property are they?' the clerk asked.

'The owner's name was Sindbad,' the captain replied, 'but from now on they will be in the charge of this passenger.'

A cry of astonishment escaped my lips, and I at once recognized him as the captain of the ship in which I had sailed on my second voyage.

'Why!' I exclaimed. 'I am Sindbad, that very merchant who many years ago was left behind on the Island of the Roc. I fell asleep there, and when I awoke I found that the ship had gone. The merchants who saw me on the Diamond Mountains and heard my adventure will bear witness that I am indeed Sindbad.'

On hearing mention of the Diamond Mountains, one of the merchants, who by this time had gathered around us, came forward and peered into my face. Then he turned to his friends, crying, 'By Allah, this is the man I once met on the Diamond Mountains, after he had been carried up from the valley by a mighty vulture! It was he who presented me with those rare diamonds.'

The captain questioned me about the contents of my bales, and I readily gave him an exact description. I also reminded him of a certain incident that had happened during our voyage, and he now recognized me and, taking me in his arms, congratulated me warmly. My goods were brought ashore, and I sold them at a substantial profit. Then we set sail and after a few days came to the land of Sind, where we also traded profitably.

In those Indian waters I saw many marvels. There was a sea monster that resembled a cow and another with a head like a donkey. I also saw a bird that hatches from a sea shell and remains floating on the water all its life.

From Sind we set sail again, and after some weeks came to Basra. I stayed there for a few days and then journeyed upstream to Baghdad, where I was joyfully welcomed by my friends and kinsmen. I gave generously to the poor and to widows and orphans, for I had returned from this voyage richer than ever before.

Tomorrow, my friends, if Allah wills, I shall tell you the story of my fourth voyage, which you will find even more extraordinary than the tales I have already related.

When the evening feast was ended, Sindbad the Sailor gave Sindbad the Porter a hundred pieces of gold, and the company took leave of their host and went their way, marveling at the wonders they had heard.

Next morning the porter returned, and when the other guests had arrived, Sindbad the Sailor began:

THE FOURTH VOYAGE
OF SINDBAD THE SAILOR

The idle and extravagant life I led after returning
to Baghdad did not make me forget the excitement
of travel in distant lands. My longing to see the
world, despite the dangers I had met, was as
strong as ever. At last I yielded to the call of the
sea and, making preparations for a long voyage,
set sail with merchandise from Basra, in the company of some well-known merchants of that port.

Helped by a favorable wind, we sailed peacefully
along, trading from port to port and from island
to island. One day a violent tempest suddenly
sprang up in mid-ocean, rolling gigantic waves as

high as mountains against our ship. We all fell on our knees in prayer and lamentation. The gale tore the sails to ribbons and snapped the mast in two; then a tremendous wave crashed down upon us from above, breaking up the vessel and tossing us all into the raging sea.

I clung fast to a floating beam, together with some of my companions who had also managed to reach it. Now paddling with our hands and feet, now swept by wind and current, we were at length thrown, half dead with cold and weariness, upon the shore of an island.

We lay down on the sand and fell asleep. Next morning we rose and made our way inland, and after a few hours came to a high building among the trees. A number of wild-looking men came out of a door and, without a word, took hold of us and led us into the building. Seated upon a throne was their King.

He ordered us to sit down, and presently his servants set before us dishes of such meat as we had never seen in all our lives. My famished companions, not noticing that the people did not eat of it themselves, devoured the meat greedily; but my own stomach revolted at the sight of the food and, in spite of my hunger, I could not eat a single mouthful. As it turned out, that abstinence saved my life, for as soon as they had swallowed the meat my friends began to lose their intelligence and to act like beasts. After a few hours of continuous feeding they became little better than savages.

While they were still eating, the natives fetched a pot of ointment, which they rubbed into the bodies of my companions. This brought about an astonishing change in their appearance: their eyes sank into their heads and their stomachs became swollen; and as the swelling increased so did their hunger.

I was horrified at this spectacle. I discovered that these barbarous men were cannibals who fattened their victims before eating them.

Robbed entirely of their human faculties, my changed companions were put into the care of a herdsman, who led them out every day to feed in the meadows. The savages lost all interest in me, for I was reduced to a shadow by hunger and fear, and my skin was soon shriveled upon my bones. One day I slipped out of my prison house and made off across the island. Away on the distant grasslands I met the herdsman with his wretched flock. But instead of chasing me or ordering me to return, he appeared to take pity on my helpless condition, and pointed to the right, as if to say, 'Go this way; fear nothing.'

I ran on and on across the plains When evening came I ate some roots and herbs and lay down on the grass to rest, but fear of the cannibals had robbed me of any wish to sleep, and at midnight I was up again and plodding painfully on. After journeying for seven days I came on the morning of the eighth toward the opposite side of the island.

I spotted human figures in the distance, and as I drew nearer found they were a party of peasants gathering pepper in a field. They crowded around me, speaking in my own language, and asked who I was and where I had come from. In reply I gave them the story of my misfortunes, and they were all amazed to hear it. They congratulated me on my escape, offered me food and water, and let me rest until evening. When their day's work was done they took me with them in a boat to their capital, which was on a neighboring island.

I was presented to their King, who received me kindly and listened with astonishment to my story. Their city, I found, was prosperous and densely populated, with many shops and markets. Many people, both rich and poor, owned fine horses, but I was surprised to see that these were ridden bareback.

During my next audience with the King I asked him why his subjects did not use a saddle and stirrups.

'Saddle?' he asked, somewhat puzzled. 'What may that be? I have never seen such a thing in all my life.'

'In that case, allow me to make one for you,' I replied. 'Then you may try it and find how comfortable and useful it can be.'

The King was pleased at my offer, and at once I looked for a skillful carpenter and instructed him to make a wooden frame for a saddle of my own design. Then I taught a blacksmith to forge a bit and a pair of stirrups. I fitted the frame with a padding of wool and leather and added a girth and tassels. When all was ready, I chose the finest of the royal horses, saddled and bridled it, and led it before the King.

He was delighted with the appearance of the new equipment, and rewarded me with a fine gift and a large sum of money. His vizier saw the saddle and begged me to make one for him. I did so; and it was not long before every courtier and nobleman in the kingdom owned a handsome saddle.

My skill soon made me the richest man on the island. The King showered honors upon me and I became a trusted courtier.

One day, as we sat chatting together in his palace, he said, 'You must know, Sindbad, that we have come to love you like a brother; we cannot bear the thought that you might someday leave our kingdom. Therefore we will ask a favor of you, which we hope you will not refuse.'

'God forbid,' I replied, 'that I should refuse you anything, Your Majesty.'

'We wish you to marry a beautiful girl who has been brought up in our court,' he said. 'She is intelligent and wealthy and will make you an excellent wife. I trust you will settle down happily with her in this city for the rest of your life. Do not refuse me this, I beg you.'

I was deeply embarrassed and did not know what to say.

'Why do you not speak, my son?' he asked.

'Your Majesty,' I faltered, 'it is my duty to obey you.'

The King sent at once for a judge and witnesses, and I was married that day to a rich woman of noble birth. The King gave us a magnificent palace and set aside for us a retinue of slaves and servants.

We lived there happily and contentedly, although in my heart of hearts I always longed to return to my own homeland with my wife, for I loved her dearly. But alas, no man can control his fate.

One day the wife of one of my closest friends died, and I went to his house to offer my condolences. Finding him overcome with grief, I tried to comfort him.

'Allah may soon give you another wife as loving and as worthy as the one he has taken from you,' I said. 'May he lighten your sorrow and prolong your life!'

But he did not raise his eyes from the ground.

'Alas,' he sighed. 'How can you wish me a long life when I have only a few hours to live?'

'Courage, my friend,' I said. 'Why do you speak of death when, thank God, you are in perfect health, sound in mind and body?'

'In a few hours,' he replied, 'I will be buried with my dead wife. It is an ancient custom in this country. When a wife dies her husband is buried with her, and if he should die first his wife is buried with him. Both must leave this world together.'

'By Allah,' I cried in horror, 'this is a most barbarous custom! How can men of sense allow such cruelty?'

While we were talking, his friends and relations, accompanied by a large crowd, came into the house and began to condole with him on the loss of his wife and his own impending death. Soon the funeral preparations were completed, and the corpse was laid upon a bier. A long procession of mourners, headed by the husband, formed outside the house and set out for the burial ground.

We all halted at the foot of a steep mound overlooking the sea. A stone was rolled away from the mouth of a deep pit, and into this pit the corpse was thrown. The band of mourners then laid hold of my friend and lowered him, by means of a long rope, into the pit, together with seven loaves of bread and a pitcher of water. The stone was rolled back and we all returned to the city.

I hastened with a heavy heart to the King's palace, and when I was admitted to his presence fell on my knees before him, crying, 'My noble master, I have visited many far countries and lived among all types of men, but in all my life I have never seen or heard of anything so barbarous as your custom of burying the living with the dead. Are strangers, like myself, obliged to conform to this custom, Your Majesty?'

'Certainly they are,' he replied. 'They, too, must

be buried with their dead wives. It is a time-honored custom that all must observe.'

At his reply I hurried home, dreading lest my wife should have died while I was out of the house. Finding her in perfect health, I comforted myself as best I could with the thought that I might one day find a way of returning to my own country, or might even die before my wife.

But things turned out otherwise. Soon afterward my wife was taken ill and in a few days died.

The King and all his courtiers came to my house to comfort me. The body of my wife was perfumed and arrayed in fine robes and rich ornaments. And when all was ready for the burial I was led behind the bier, at the head of a long procession.

We came to the mound. The stone was lifted from the mouth of the pit and the body of my wife thrown in. The mourners gathered around me to say farewell, paying no attention to my cries. They tied me with a long rope and lowered me into the pit, with the customary loaves and a pitcher of water. Then they rolled back the stone and went their way.

When I touched the bottom of the pit I found myself in a vast cavern filled with bones. I threw myself upon the earth, crying, 'You deserve this fate, Sindbad! Here you will pay the final penalty for your ambition and greed! Why did you marry on this island? If only you had died on the bare mountains or perished in the sea!'

But the love of life still glowed within me, and after some time I unfastened the loaves and pitcher of water, and ate and drank a little.

For several days I lived on my provisions, and when they were finished I prepared myself to die. I had become resigned to my fate, when one day I heard a sound of movement near by. Springing to my feet, I followed the noise closely until I could faintly see the form of some animal scurrying before me. As I ran in pursuit of the creature, stumbling here and there in the dark, I gradually made out at the far side of the cavern a speck of light that grew larger and brighter as I advanced toward it. When I reached the end of the cave the fleeing animal disappeared. To my great joy, I realized I had come upon a tunnel that the wild beasts had burrowed from the other side of the mound. I scrambled into this tunnel, crawling on all fours, and soon reached the opening. I was at the foot of a high cliff, with the blue sky and the yellow sand before me.

I fell upon my knees in prayer and thanked the Almighty for my escape. The warm and wholesome air breathed new life into my veins. I rejoiced to see again the loveliness of earth and sky.

Strengthened with hope and courage, I made my way back along the tunnel and gathered up all the jewels, pearls, and precious ornaments that I could find in the cave. These I fastened into bales and carried to the seashore, where I remained scanning the horizon until nightfall. Next morning, as I was sitting beneath a rock, praying for a speedy rescue, I saw a sail far off upon the sea. Hoisting my turban on a stick, I waved it frantically about as I ran up and down the beach. The ship's crew saw my signal and at once sent a boat to fetch me.

'How did you find your way to this wild spot?' asked the captain in astonishment. 'I have never seen a living man here in all my days.'

'Sir,' I replied, 'I was shipwrecked off this shore many days ago. These bales are the remnants of my goods that I managed to save.' I kept the truth from him lest there should be some on board who were citizens of that island.

From one of my packages I took out a rare pearl and offered it to him. 'Please accept this,' I said, 'as a reward for saving my life.'

But the captain politely refused the gift. 'It is not our custom,' he said, 'to accept payment for a good deed. We have rescued many a voyager, fed him and clothed him, and finally set him ashore with a little present of our own besides. Allah alone is the giver of rewards.'

I thanked him with all my heart and called down blessings upon him. Then the ship resumed its voyage. As we sailed from island to island and from sea to sea, I eagerly looked forward to seeing my native land again. At times, however, the thought of that terrible cavern would come back to me and make me shudder.

At last we arrived safely in Basra. I stayed there

for a few days, then sailed up the river to Baghdad. Loaded with treasure, I hastened to my own house, where I was joyfully welcomed by my friends and relatives. I sold the precious stones for a fabulous sum and gave generously to widows and orphans.

That is the story of my fourth voyage. Tomorrow, if Allah wills, I shall give you an account of my fifth voyage.

After the evening feast, Sindbad the Sailor gave Sindbad the Porter a hundred pieces of gold. The company took leave of their host and went their way, marveling at all they had heard. Next morning the porter returned, and when all the other guests had assembled, Sindbad the Sailor began:

THE FIFTH VOYAGE
OF SINDBAD THE SAILOR

Know, my friends, that the merry and peaceful life I led after my return soon made me forget my sufferings in the Land of the Cannibals and in the Cavern of the Dead. I remembered only the pleasures of adventure and the considerable gains that my travels had earned me, and once again longed to sail new seas and explore new lands. So I equipped myself with goods suitable for selling in foreign countries, packed them up in bales, and took them to Basra.

One day I saw from the wharf a newly built ship with tall masts and fine sails that caught my fancy. I bought her outright and filled her with my merchandise. Then I hired an experienced captain and a well-trained crew, and accepted as passengers several other merchants who offered to pay their passages in advance.

Blessed with a favorable wind, we voyaged many days and nights, trading from sea to sea and from shore to shore, and came at length to a desert island. Here we caught sight of a solitary white dome, half buried in the sand. This I recognized at once as a roc's egg; and the passengers begged leave to land, so as to get a closer look at it.

As ill luck would have it, some of the merchants were thoughtless enough to throw stones at the egg. When the shell was broken, they decided to have a feast, dragged out the young bird, and cut it up in pieces. They returned on board to tell me of their adventure.

I was filled with horror and cried, 'We are lost! The parent birds will now pursue our ship and destroy us all!'

Scarcely had I finished speaking when the sun was suddenly hidden from our view as by a great cloud, and the world grew dark around us as the two rocs came flying home. On finding their egg broken and their young one destroyed, they uttered deafening cries, took to the air again, and soon vanished from sight.

'All aboard, quickly!' I shouted. 'We must flee from this island at once.'

The captain weighed anchor and with all speed

we sailed toward the open sea. But before long the world grew dark again, and in the ominous twilight we could see the gigantic birds hovering overhead, each carrying in its talons an enormous rock. When they were directly above us, one of them dropped its load, which narrowly missed the ship and opened such a chasm in the ocean that for a moment we could see the sandy bottom. The waves rose mountain high, tossing us up and down. Presently the other bird dropped its rock and this time hit its mark. Those of us who were not crushed to death were hurled into the sea and swept away by the giant waves.

Through the grace of Allah I managed to cling to a floating piece of wreckage. Sitting astride this, I paddled with my feet and, aided by wind and current, at last reached the shore of an island.

I threw myself upon the sand and lay down for a while to recover my breath. Then I rose and wandered about the island, which was as beautiful as the Garden of Eden. The air was filled with the singing of birds, and wherever I turned, I saw trees loaded with luscious fruit or crystal brooks meandering among banks of flowers. I refreshed myself with the fruit and water and, when evening came, lay down upon the grass.

Early next morning I set off to explore the island. After a long stroll among the trees I came to a little stream. On the bank sat a gray-haired old man. His body was covered with a cloak of leaves.

Taking him for a shipwrecked voyager like myself, I greeted him in my own language; but he replied only with a mournful nod. When I asked him how he came to be there, instead of answering he begged me with signs to take him upon my shoulder and carry him across the brook. I readily bent down, lifted him upon my back, and waded through the stream. On reaching the opposite bank I stooped again for him to get off; but instead of alighting, the old wretch powerfully threw his legs, which I now saw were covered with a rough black skin like a buffalo's, around my neck and crossed them tightly over my chest. Seized with fear, I desperately tried to shake him off, but the monster pressed his thighs tighter and tighter around my throat until I could no longer breathe. The world darkened before my eyes and with a choking cry I dropped unconscious to the ground.

When I came to, I found the old monster still crouching upon my shoulders, although he had now sufficiently relaxed his hold to let me breathe. As soon as he saw that I had recovered my senses, he pushed one foot against my belly and, violently kicking my side with the other, forced me to get up and walk under some trees. Leisurely he plucked the fruits and ate them. Every time I halted against his will or failed to do his bidding he kicked me hard, so that I had no choice but to obey him. All day long he remained seated on my shoulders; I was no better than a beast of burden.

At night he made me lie down, but never for one moment loosened his hold around my neck. Next morning he roused me with a kick and ordered me to carry him among the trees.

Day after day he stayed glued to my back, driving me pitilessly from glade to glade. I cursed the charitable instinct that had prompted me to help him, and longed for death to deliver me from my evil plight.

After many weeks of miserable slavery I chanced one day to come upon a field where gourds were growing in abundance. I picked up one large gourd, which was sun-dried and empty, cleaned it thoroughly, and squeezed into it the juice of several bunches of grapes; then, carefully stopping the hole that I had cut into its shell, I left the juice in the sun to ferment.

Returning with the old man a few days afterward, I found the gourd filled with the purest wine. The drink gave me new strength, and I began to feel so light and cheerful that I went tripping merrily among the trees, scarcely aware of my hateful burden.

Noticing the effect of the wine, my captor asked me to let him taste it. I did not dare refuse. He took the gourd from my hand, raised it to his lips, and gulped down the liquor to the dregs. Soon, overcome with the wine, he began to sway from side to side, and his legs gradually relaxed their hold around my neck. With one violent jerk of my shoulders I hurled him to the ground, where he lay motionless. Then I quickly picked up a great stone from among the trees and fell upon the fiend with all my strength. That was the end of my tormentor; may Allah have no mercy on him!

Overjoyed at my new freedom, I roamed the island for many weeks, eating of its fruit and drinking from its springs. One day, however, as I sat on the shore thinking about the ups and downs of my life and recalling memories of my native land, I saw, to my great joy, a sail heading toward the island. On reaching land the vessel anchored, and the passengers came ashore to fill their pitchers with water.

I ran in haste to meet them. They were greatly astonished to see me and gathered around, asking who I was and where I came from. I told them all that had befallen me since my arrival, and they replied, 'It is a marvel that you have escaped alive, for the monster who crouched on your shoulders was none other than the Old Man of the Sea. Praise be to Allah for your deliverance!'

They took me to their ship. The captain received me kindly and listened with astonishment to my adventure. Then we set sail, and after many days and nights cast anchor in the harbor of a city perched on a high cliff, and known among travelers as the City of Apes on account of the multitude of monkeys that infested it by night.

I went ashore with one of the merchants from the ship and wandered about the town in search of some employment. Soon we fell in with a crowd of men who were on their way to the gates leading out of the city. They had sacks of pebbles on their shoulders. My friend the merchant gave me a large cotton bag and said, 'Fill this with pebbles and follow these people into the forest. Do exactly as they do, and thus you will earn your livelihood.'

I filled the sack with pebbles and joined the crowd. The merchant recommended me to them, saying, 'Here is a shipwrecked stranger; teach him to earn his bread and Allah will reward you.'

When we had marched a great distance from the city we came to a vast valley, covered with coconut trees so straight and tall that no man could ever climb them. As we drew nearer I saw among the trees innumerable monkeys. They fled at our approach and swiftly climbed up to the fruit-laden fronds.

My companions now set down their bags and began to pelt the monkeys with pebbles; and I did the same. The tormented animals retaliated by pelting us with coconuts, and these we gathered up and put into our sacks. When they were full we returned to the city and sold the nuts in the market place.

Thereafter I went every day to the forest with the coconut hunters and traded profitably with the fruit. When I had saved enough money for my homeward voyage, I said good-by to my friend the merchant and embarked in a vessel bound for

Basra, taking with me a large cargo of coconuts and other produce.

In the course of our voyage we put in at many heathen islands, where I sold some of my coconuts at a substantial profit and exchanged others for cinnamon, pepper, and Chinese aloe. On reaching the Sea of Pearls, I engaged several divers who, in a short time, brought up a large quantity of priceless pearls.

After that we set sail again. Voyaging many days and nights, we arrived at last in Basra. I spent a few days in that town and then, loaded with treasure, set out for Baghdad.

I was glad to be back in my native city. Hastening to my old street, I entered my own house, where all my friends and kinsmen gathered to greet me. I gave them gold and many presents, and distributed a large sum in charity among widows and orphans.

That is the story of my fifth voyage. Tomorrow, my friends, if Allah wills, I shall tell you the tale of my sixth voyage.

The evening feast came to an end. Sindbad the Sailor gave Sindbad the Porter a hundred pieces of gold, and the company departed, marveling at all they had heard. Next morning the porter returned, and when the other guests had arrived, Sindbad the Sailor began:

THE SIXTH VOYAGE
OF SINDBAD THE SAILOR

One day I was sitting peacefully and comfortably at home, when a band of merchants who had returned from abroad called on me to give me news of foreign lands. At the sight of these travelers I remembered the joy of returning from a far journey to be united with friends and kinsmen after a long absence and soon afterward I made ready for another voyage and left Basra with a rich cargo.

We sailed many days and nights, buying and selling wherever the ship anchored and exploring the unfamiliar places at which we called. One day, as we were sailing in mid-ocean, we heard a loud cry from the captain. He beat himself about the face, tore at his beard, and hurled his turban onto the deck. We gathered around him, asking what had gone wrong.

'Alas, we are lost!' he cried. 'We have been driven off our course into an unknown ocean, where nothing can save us from final wreck but Allah's mercy. Let us pray to him!'

Then, while some passengers fell on their knees praying and others were bidding each other farewell, the captain climbed the mast to trim the sails. Scarcely had he reached the top than we were swept up in a violent squall, which dashed the ship against a craggy shore at the foot of a high cliff. The vessel split to pieces and we were all flung into the raging sea. Some were drowned, while others, like myself, managed to survive by clinging to the jutting rocks.

Scattered all along the shore were the remains of other wrecks, and the sands were strewn with countless bales from which rare merchandise and costly ornaments had broken loose. I wandered among these treasures for many hours and then, winding my way through the rocks, suddenly came upon a river that flowed from a gorge in the mountain. I followed its course with my eyes and was surprised to find that, instead of running into the sea, the river plunged into a vast rocky cavern and disappeared. The banks were covered with jewels, and I could see that the bed was studded with rubies, emeralds, and other precious stones. The entire river glowed with a fiery brilliance.

Meanwhile, the others who had escaped drowning lay in a sad plight on the shore, counting the days as they dragged by and waiting for the approach of death. One by one my companions died as they came to the end of their food, and we who survived buried them. Eventually I was left quite alone.

When I realized that death was near, I lay down on the cold earth and gave myself up to utter despair. 'Why,' I cried, 'oh, why was I not content to be safe and happy in Baghdad? Had I not enough riches to last me twice a lifetime?'

Rousing myself at last, I wandered again to the river. As I watched it plunge into the cavern, I struck upon a plan.

'By Allah,' I thought, 'this river must have both a beginning and an end. If it enters the mountain on this side, it must somehow emerge into daylight again; and if I could follow its course, the current might in the end bring me to some inhabited land. If I am destined to survive this, Allah will guide me to safety; if I perish, it will not be worse than the miserable fate of starving to death that awaits me here.'

Encouraged by these thoughts, I collected a few large branches, laid them on some planks from the wrecked vessels and bound them with some cables into a raft. This I loaded with sacks of rubies, pearls, and other stones; then, commending myself to Allah, I launched the raft upon the water and jumped aboard.

The fast current carried me along, and I soon found myself in the brooding darkness of the cavern. My raft began to bump violently against the jagged sides, while the passage grew smaller and smaller, until I was compelled to lie flat on my stomach for fear of striking my head. It was not long before I was wishing that I could return to the open shore. But the current became faster and faster as the river swept headlong down its channel, and I resigned myself to certain death. Overcome by terror and fatigue, I sank at last into a heavy sleep.

I cannot tell how long I slept, but when I woke I found I was lying on my raft close to the riverbank, under the open sky. The river was flowing gently through a stretch of pleasant meadowland, and on the bank stood Indians and Abyssinians.

As soon as these men saw that I was awake, they gathered about me, asking questions in a language I did not understand. Presently one of them came forward and greeted me in my own tongue.

'Who may you be,' he asked, 'and where have you come from? We were working in our field when we saw you drifting down the river. We secured your raft to the bank and, not wishing to wake you, left you here in safety. Now tell us, what accident cast you on this river that flows from under the mountain?'

I begged them first to give me some food, and promised to answer all their questions after I had eaten. They brought me a variety of meats, and when I had regained my strength a little I gave an account of all that had happened to me since my shipwreck. My miraculous escape so astonished them that they insisted on taking me to their King, so that I might tell him of my adventure.

Carrying my raft with all its contents upon their shoulders, they led me to their city. The King received me courteously and listened in profound astonishment to my story. Opening my treasures in his presence, I laid at his feet a priceless choice of emeralds, pearls, and rubies. In return he conferred upon me the highest honors of the kingdom and invited me to stay at the palace as his guest.

I rose rapidly in the King's favor and soon became a trusted courtier. One day he asked me about my country and its far-famed Caliph. I praised the wisdom, piety, and goodness of Harun al-Rashid and spoke at length of his glorious deeds. The King was deeply impressed by my account.

'This monarch,' he said, 'must indeed be a great man. We desire to send a present worthy of him, and appoint you the bearer.'

'I hear and obey,' I replied. 'I will gladly deliver your gift to the Commander of the Faithful, and will inform him that in Your Majesty he has a worthy ally and a trusted friend.'

The King gave orders that a magnificent present be prepared, and a new ship was built for the voyage. When all was ready for departure, I presented myself at the royal palace, thanked the King for the favors he had shown me, and took leave of him and his courtiers.

Then I set sail, and after many days arrived safely in Basra. I hastened to Baghdad with the royal gift, and when I had been admitted to the Caliph's presence I kissed the ground before him and told him of my mission. Al-Rashid marveled at my adventure and gave orders that the story be written on parchment in letters of gold, so that it might be kept among the treasures of the kingdom.

Then I hurried to my old street and entered my own house, where I rejoiced to meet my people. I gave them gold and costly presents, and distributed alms among the poor of the city.

Such is the story of my sixth voyage. Tomorrow, if Allah wills, I shall recount to you the tale of my seventh and last voyage.

When the evening feast was ended, Sindbad the Sailor gave Sindbad the Porter a hundred pieces of gold, and the guests departed, marveling at all they had heard.

Next morning the porter returned, and when the other guests had assembled, Sindbad the Sailor began:

THE LAST VOYAGE
OF SINDBAD THE SAILOR

For many years after my return I lived happily in Baghdad, feasting with my favorite companions and squandering the riches that my travels had earned me. But though I was now past the prime of life, my spirit was still untamed and once more I longed to see the world and travel in the lands of men. I boarded a good ship in company with some eminent merchants, and set sail with a fair wind and a rich cargo.

We voyaged peacefully for many weeks, but one day, while we were sailing in the China Seas, a violent gale arose. The rain came down in torrents.

Quickly we covered our bales with canvas to protect them, while the captain climbed up the mast and scanned the horizon in all directions. After a few moments he came down trembling with fear.

'Pray to Allah,' he cried, 'that he may deliver us from the peril into which we have fallen! Say your farewells, for the wind has driven us off our course into the world's farthermost seas!'

Opening one of his cabin chests, the captain took from it a small cotton bag filled with an ashlike powder. He sprinkled some water over the powder and inhaled it into his nostrils; then, opening a little book, he intoned some magic charms and turned to us, saying, 'Know that we are now approaching the very edge of the world. Here the land teems with serpents of extraordinary size, and the sea is filled with giant whales that can swallow vessels whole. Farewell, my friends; and may Allah have mercy upon us!'

Scarcely had he finished speaking than the ship was tossed high in the air, then flung back into the sea. An ear-splitting cry, more terrible than thunder, boomed through the swelling ocean. Terror seized our hearts as we saw a gigantic whale, as big as a mountain, rush swiftly toward us, followed by another just as big, and a third greater than the two put together. This last monster leaped from the surging waves, opened its enormous mouth, and seized in its jaws the ship with all its contents. I ran quickly to the edge of the tilting deck and, casting off my clothes, jumped into the sea just before the whale swallowed the ship and vanished under the foam with its two companions.

With Allah's help, I clung to a piece of timber that had fallen from the lost vessel and, after struggling with the waves for two days and nights, was thrown upon an island covered with fruit trees and watered by many streams. I wandered aimlessly about the coast and soon came to a fast-flowing river. I hit upon the idea of building a raft and allowing myself to be carried downstream by the current, as I had done on my last voyage 'If I succeed in saving myself this time,' I said, 'all will be well with me and I solemnly vow never again to let the thought of voyaging enter my mind. If I fail, I shall at least find rest from the troubles and trials that my folly has earned me.'

I made the raft by cutting branches from a tree and fastening them together with the stems of creeping plants. I loaded it with fruit and, putting my trust in Allah, pushed off down the river.

For three days and nights the current carried me along so swiftly that I became weak and dazed, and eventually sank into unconsciousness. When I came to, I found myself heading toward a steep decline down which the waters of the river tumbled in a mighty cataract. I clung with all my strength to the branches of the raft and prayed silently for a merciful end. It was at the very brink of the waterfall that I suddenly felt the raft halted in its course and saw that I was caught in a net that a group of men had thrown from the bank. The raft was quickly hauled to land, and I was released from the net half dead with terror and fatigue.

As I lay on the mud, I gradually became aware of an old man bending over me. He greeted me kindly and wrapped me in warm garments, and when my strength had returned a little he helped me to my feet and led me slowly to the city baths. There I was washed with perfumed water, and then the old man took me to his own house, where I was given an excellent meal. After the feast, slaves washed my hands and wiped them on napkins of silk. In the evening my host conducted me to a beautiful room, ordered several of his slaves to wait upon me, and wished me good night.

The kind old man entertained me in this way for three days. When I was completely recovered he came to see me in my room and sat talking with me for an hour. Just before leaving my room, however, he turned and said, 'If you wish to sell your goods, my friend, I will gladly go down with you to the market.'

I was puzzled by this remark and did not know what to say. What goods was he talking about?

'Do not worry about them, my son,' he went on. 'If we receive a good offer, we will sell them; if not, I will keep them for you in my own storehouse until they fetch a better price.'

Hiding my bewilderment, I replied, 'I am willing to do whatever you suggest.'

With this I got up and went with him to the market. There I saw an excited crowd admiring an object on the ground with exclamations of the highest praise. Pushing my way among the merchants, I was astonished to find that the center of attention was none other than the raft on which I had sailed down the river. Presently the old man ordered a broker to begin the auction.

'Who will make the first bid for this precious sandalwood?' began the broker. 'Come along, my friends. Have you ever in all your lives seen finer sandalwood than this?'

'A hundred pieces of gold!' one of the merchants cried.

'A thousand!' another shouted.

'Eleven hundred!' my host exclaimed.

'Agreed,' I nodded.

Upon this, the old man ordered his slaves to carry the wood to his warehouse. When he got home he took me to his private chamber and paid me eleven hundred pieces of gold.

One day, as we sat talking, he suddenly asked, 'My son, will you do me a great favor?'

'With all my heart,' I replied, 'if I have the power to do it.'

'I am a very old man,' he said, 'and have no son of my own. Yet I have a young and beautiful daughter, who on my death will be mistress of my entire fortune. If you will have her for your wife, you will inherit my wealth and become chief of the merchants of this city.'

I readily agreed to the proposal. A sumptuous feast was held, a judge and witnesses were called in, and I was married to the old man's daughter amid great rejoicings. When the wedding guests were gone I was conducted to the bridal room, where I was allowed to see my wife for the first time. I found her very beautiful.

We grew to love each other dearly and lived together in happiness and contentment. Not long afterward my wife's father died, and I inherited all his property. His slaves became my slaves and his goods my goods, and the merchants of the city appointed me their chief in his place.

One day I was surprised by a strange event that apparently took place annually. The men of that land, for a whole day each year, suffered a wondrous change in their bodies. They grew wings on their shoulders and flew high up in the air, leaving their wives and children behind. I was amazed at this occurrence, and begged one of my friends to let me cling to him when he next took his flight. He promised to grant my request, and when the long-awaited day arrived, I took a tight hold of my friend's waist and was at once carried up swiftly in the air. We climbed higher and higher into the void until I could hear the angels in their choirs singing under the vault of heaven. Moved with awe, I cried, 'Glory and praise to Allah, Lord of the Creation!'

The words were scarcely out of my mouth when my flying companion dropped down through the air and alighted on the top of a desolate mountain. There, to my surprise, he threw me off his back and took to the air again, calling curses on my head.

As I sat thinking what I should do, I saw two youths approaching me. Their faces shone with an unearthly beauty, and each held a staff of red gold in his hand. I rose to my feet and wished them peace. They returned my greeting courteously.

'Who are you, and what brought you to this barren mountain?' I asked.

'We are worshipers of the true God,' they replied. And so saying, one of the youths pointed to a path on the mountain, handed me his gold staff, and led the way with his companion.

Bewildered at these words, I set out in the direction he indicated, leaning upon the staff as I walked. I had not gone far when I saw coming toward me the flier who had so roughly set me down upon the mountaintop. I went up to him and said gently, 'Is this how friends behave toward friends?'

The winged man, who was no longer angry, replied, 'Know that my fall was caused by your unfortunate mention of your god. The word has this effect upon us, and this is why we never utter it.'

I assured him that I had meant no harm and promised to commit no such offense in future. Then I begged him to carry me home. He took me upon his shoulders and in a few moments set me down before my house.

My wife was overjoyed at my return, and when I told her of my adventure, she said, 'We must no longer stay among these people. Know that they are the brothers of Satan and have no knowledge of the true God.'

'How was it, then, that your father lived among them?' I asked.

'My father belonged to a different race,' she replied. 'He believed in none of their creeds and did not lead their life. As he is now dead, let us sell our property and leave this blasphemous land.'

And so I made up my mind to return home. We sold our houses and estates, hired a vessel, and set sail with a rich cargo.

Aided by a favorable wind, we voyaged many days and nights and at last came to Basra and thence to Baghdad, the City of Peace. I carried to my stores the valuables I had brought with me and, taking my wife to my own house in my old street, rejoiced to meet my people. They told me that this voyage had kept me abroad for nearly twenty-seven years, and marveled exceedingly at my adventures.

I gave profound thanks to Allah for bringing me safely home, and solemnly vowed never to travel again by sea or land. Such, dear guests, was the longest and last of my voyages.

*

When the evening feast was over, Sindbad the Sailor gave Sindbad the Porter a hundred pieces of gold, which he took with thanks and blessings. Then he went his way, marveling at all he had heard.

The porter remained a frequent visitor to the house of his famous friend, and the two lived in happiness and peace until the end of their lives.

The Tale of Maaruf the Cobbler

Once upon a time, there lived in the city of Cairo a poor and honest cobbler who earned his living by patching old shoes.

He was married to an ugly woman called Fatimah, nicknamed by her neighbors the 'Shrew' because of her quarrelsome disposition and her scolding tongue. She treated her husband cruelly, cursing him a thousand times a day and making his life a burden and a torment. Maaruf feared her malice and dreaded her fiery temper. He was a quiet, sensitive man and was ever anxious to avoid a scene.

One day his wife came to him and said, 'See

that you bring me a butter cake tonight, and let it be dripping with honey.'

'May Allah send me good business today,' the cobbler replied, 'and you shall gladly have one. At present I have not a single copper, but the bounty of Allah is great.'

'Talk not to me of Allah's bounty!' rejoined the shrew. 'If you do not bring back a butter cake, dripping with honey, I will make your day blacker than the night!'

'Allah is merciful!' sighed Maaruf.

He left the house and went to open his shop, saying, 'O Lord, grant me this day the means to buy a honey cake for my wife, that I may save myself from her fury!'

As ill luck would have it, no customer entered his shop all day and he did not earn enough even for a loaf of bread. In the evening he locked the shop and walked along the street. He came to a pastry cook's, and as he gazed sadly at the confections in the window, his eyes filled with tears. Noticing his dejected look, the pastry cook called out to him, 'Why so sad, Maaruf? Come in, and tell me your trouble.'

When the cook heard the cause of the cobbler's unhappiness, he laughed and said, 'No harm shall come to you, my friend. How much butter cake do you wish to have?'

'Five ounces,' muttered Maaruf.

'Gladly,' said the cook. 'You can pay me some other time.'

He cut a large slice, and added, 'I fear I have no honey, only sugar-cane syrup. I assure you it is just as good.'

He poured syrup and melted butter over the cake until it was worthy of a king's table. Then he handed the cake to the cobbler, together with a cheese and a loaf of bread for his supper. Maaruf could scarcely find words to thank the good man. He called down blessings upon him, and went home.

As soon as his wife saw him she demanded, 'Have you brought me the butter cake?' Maaruf placed it before her.

In a loud, menacing voice she cried, 'Did I not tell you it must be made with honey? You have brought me a syrup cake to spite me! Did you think I would not know the difference?'

Maaruf humbly stammered his explanation. 'Good wife, I did not buy this cake,' he said. 'It was given me on credit by a kind hearted pastry cook.'

'These excuses will not help you!' shrieked the furious woman. 'There, take your miserable syrup dish!'

And she flung the cake in her husband's face and ordered him to go and fetch her another made with honey. Then she dealt him a savage blow that knocked out one of his teeth.

Losing all patience, Maaraf lifted his hand and gave the woman a mild slap on the head. At this she flew into a desperate rage, gripped his beard with both her hands, and, raising her voice to its loudest pitch, shrieked, 'Help, good people! Help! My husband is murdering me!'

The neighbors heard her cries and came rushing into the house. After a struggle they managed to free the cobbler's beard from her clutches, but when they saw his injury and heard the cause of the dispute they rebuked her and tried to reason with her.

'We are all content to eat syrup cake, and indeed find it as good as the other kind,' they said. 'What has your poor husband done that you should torment him so?'

Unable to bear with his wife any more, the long-suffering cobbler made up his mind to run away. He left the house, and trudged dolefully toward the city gates. It was a bleak winter evening, and as he came out of the town and found himself among the garbage heaps, the rain began to fail in torrents, drenching him to the skin. On and on he ran, and at nightfall came to a ruined hovel where he took shelter from the storm. He sat on the ground and wept bitterly.

'How shall I save myself from this fiend?' he cried. 'O Allah, help me to fly to some far-off land, where I shall never see her again!'

While he was saying this the wall of the hovel suddenly opened and a tall and fearsome jinnee appeared before him.

'Son of Adam,' roared the jinnee, 'what calamity

can have befallen you that you disturb my slumbers with your wailing? I am the jinnee of this ruin and have dwelt here these hundred years; yet never have I seen the like of this behaviour.'

But he was not as evil as he looked. Moved with pity, he said, 'Tell me what you desire, and I will do your bidding.'

Maaruf told him his unhappy story.

'Mount on my back,' said the jinnee, 'and I will take you to a land where your wife will never find you.'

So the cobbler climbed onto the back of the jinnee, who flew with him between earth and sky all night, and at daybreak set him down on the top of a mountain.

'Son of Adam,' said the jinnee, 'go down this mountain and you will come to the gates of Ikhtiyan-al-Khatan. In that city you will find refuge from your wife.'

And so saying, he vanished. Amazed and bewildered, Maaruf remained until sunrise on the spot where the jinnee left him. Then he climbed down the mountain and at length came to the walls of a city. He entered the gates and walked through the streets. The townsfolk stared at him with wondering eyes and gathered about him, marveling at his strange costume. Presently a man stepped forward and asked where he had come from.

'From Cairo,' Maaraf replied.

'When did you leave Cairo?' the man asked.

'Last night,' he answered, 'just after dark.'

At these words his questioner laughed incredulously and turned to the bystanders. 'Listen to this madman! He tells us he left Cairo only last night!'

The crowd greeted this remark with laughter and pressed around Maaruf. 'Have you lost your senses?' some asked. 'How can it be that you left Cairo only last night? Do you not know that Cairo is at least a year's journey from here?'

Maaruf swore that he was speaking the truth and, to prove his story, took from his pocket a loaf of Cairo bread and held it up to them to see. All were astonished to see the loaf, which was of a kind unknown in their country and was still soft and fresh. A few believed the stranger, while others ridiculed him. As this was going on, a well-dressed merchant, followed by two slaves, came riding by. He stopped near the crowd and rebuked them sternly.

'Are you not ashamed to make fun of this man?' he said.

Then, turning to Maaruf, he spoke to him kindly and invited him to his house.

There his host dressed Maaruf in a merchant's robe worth a thousand pieces of gold, seated him in a splendid hall, and entertained him to an excellent meal. When they had finished eating, the merchant said to the cobbler, 'Tell me, brother, what land you have come from. By your dress, you would seem to be an Egyptian.'

'You are right, master,' replied Maaruf. 'I am an Egyptian, and Cairo is the city of my birth.'

'What is your trade?' the merchant asked.

'I am a cobbler: I patch old shoes.'

'Whereabouts in Cairo do you live?'

'In Red Lane,' Maaruf replied.

'What folk do you know there?'

Maaruf named several of his neighbors in that street.

'Do you know Sheikh Ahmad the perfume seller?' asked the merchant eagerly.

'Do I know him?' Maaruf laughed. 'Why, he is my next-door neighbor!'

'How is he keeping?'

'Allah be thanked, he is in the best of health,' the cobbler replied.

'How many sons has he now?'

'He has three sons: Mustapha, Mohammed, and Ali.'

'What do they do for a living?' inquired the host.

'The eldest, Mustapha,' replied Maaruf, 'is a schoolmaster. Mohammed, the second, is a perfume seller and has set up a shop of his own next to his father's. As for Ali, he was the playmate of my childhood – and a couple of mischievous little rogues we certainly were. Together we would enter the mosques and steal the prayer books; then we would sell them in the market and buy sweets with the money. One day someone caught us red-handed and complained to our parents.

Sheikh Ahmad gave his son a thrashing and poor little Ali ran away from home. No news has been heard of him these twenty years.'

Here the merchant threw his arms around the cobbler's neck and wept for joy.

'Praise be to Allah!' he cried. 'O Maaruf, I am that very Ali, the son of Sheikh Ahmad the perfume seller.'

Then Ali asked his friend what had brought him to Ikhtiyan-al-Khatan, and the cobbler recounted all that happened to him since his disastrous marriage. He explained how he had chosen to flee the city rather than remain at the mercy of his wife, how he met the jinnee in the ruined hovel, and how he was carried overnight to that city.

Maaruf now asked his friend how he had risen to such prosperity.

'After I left Cairo,' said Ali, 'I wandered for many years from place to place and at last arrived, alone and friendless, in this city. I found the people honest and kindhearted, hospitable to strangers and always ready to help the poor. I told them – God forgive me! – that I was a rich merchant, the owner of a great caravan that would shortly arrive in their city. They gave me a splendid mansion for my use and lent me a thousand pieces of gold. With this money I bought a quantity of goods and sold them the next day at a profit of fifty pieces. I bought more goods, and, to make myself better known, sought the acquaintance of the richest merchants in the town and entertained them lavishly in my house. I continued to buy and sell until I had amassed a large fortune.

'Now, my friend, if you tell the people of this city that you are a poor cobbler, that you have run away from a nagging wife, and that you left Cairo only yesterday, no one will believe you and you will become the laughingstock of the whole town. If you tell them you were carried here by a jinnee, you will frighten everyone away and they will think, "The man is possessed of an evil spirit." No, my friend, this will not do.'

'Then what am I to do?' asked the perplexed Maaruf.

'Tomorrow morning,' said Ali, 'you will mount my finest mule and ride to the market with one of my slaves walking behind you all the way. There you will find me sitting among the richest merchants of the city. When I see you I will rise and greet you. I will kiss your hand and receive you with the utmost respect. After you have taken your seat among the other merchants, I shall ask you about many kinds of merchandise, saying, "Have you such-and-such a cloth?" And you must answer, "Plenty! Plenty!" When they ask me who you are, I will say you are a merchant of great wealth, and praise your generosity. If a beggar holds out his hand to you, you must give him gold. In this way you will earn the respect of the merchants. They will seek to know you and to trade with you, and before long you will indeed become a merchant of great wealth.'

Seeing no other way out of his predicament, Maaruf reluctantly agreed to his friend's plan. Next morning, Ali clothed him magnificently, gave him a thousand gold pieces, and mounted him upon his best mule. At the appointed time the cobbler rode to the market, where he found his friend sitting among the merchants. As soon as Ali saw him approaching he bowed low and threw himself at his feet. He kissed his hand, and helped him from his mule. 'May your day be blessed, great Maaruf!' he said.

When the newcomer had gravely taken his seat, the wondering merchants came to Ali one by one and asked in a low voice, 'Who may this sheikh be?'

'He is one of the chief merchants of Egypt,' Ali replied. 'His wealth and the wealth of his father and forefathers are of proverbial fame. He possesses shops and storehouses in all corners of the earth, and his agents and partners are the pillars of commerce in every city of the East. Indeed, the wealthiest merchant in our town is but a poor peddler when compared with him.'

Hearing this praise, the merchants thronged around Maaruf, vying with each other to welcome him. The chief of the merchants himself came to greet him and questioned him eagerly about the goods he had brought.

'Doubtless, sir,' he said, 'you have many bales of yellow silk?'

'Plenty! Plenty!' answered Maaruf, without a moment's hesitation.

'And blood-red damask?' asked another.

'Plenty! Plenty!' the cobbler replied.

To all their questions he made the same answer, and when one of the merchants begged him to show them a few samples, Maaruf replied, 'Certainly, as soon as my caravan arrives.'

He explained to the company that he was expecting a caravan of a thousand mules within the next few days.

Now while the merchants were chatting and marveling at the extraordinary richness of the caravan they would soon be seeing, a beggar came forward and held out his hand to each in turn. One or two gave him a silver piece, some a copper, but most of them turned him away.

Maaruf calmly drew out a handful of gold and gave it to the beggar.

The merchants raised their eyebrows and thought to themselves, 'By Allah! this man must be richer than a king!'

Then a poor woman approached him, and to her also he gave a handful of gold. Scarcely believing her eyes, the woman hurried away to tell the other beggars, and they all came flocking around Maaruf with outstretched hands. The cobbler gave each a handful of gold, until the thousand pieces were finished.

'By Allah,' he said, 'to think there are so many beggars in this city! Had I known, I would have come prepared, for it is not my way to refuse money. What shall I do now if a beggar comes to me before my caravan arrives? If only I had, say, a thousand pieces of gold!'

'Do not let that trouble you,' said the chief of the merchants.

He sent at once for a thousand gold pieces and handed the money to Maaruf. The cobbler continued to hand out gold to every beggar who passed by. When the muezzin's call summoned the faithful to afternoon prayers, he went with the merchants to the mosque, and what remained of the thousand pieces he threw over the heads of the worshipers.

As soon as the prayers were over he borrowed another thousand and these also he scattered among the poor. By nightfall Maaruf had obtained five thousand gold pieces from the merchants and given them all away, while his friend Ali, horrified at this extravagance, watched the proceedings helplessly. And to all his creditors the cobbler said, 'When my caravan arrives, if you want gold, you shall have gold; and if you want goods, you shall have goods, for I have vast quantities of them.'

That night Ali entertained the merchants at his house. Maaruf spoke of nothing but jewels and rich silks, and whenever they asked him if he had this or that merchandise in his caravan, he replied, 'Plenty! Plenty!'

Next morning he again, went to the market, talked to the merchants about his caravan, and borrowed more money to give away. By the end of twenty days he had taken sixty thousand pieces of gold on credit. And still no caravan arrived – no, not so much as a one-eyed mule.

At last the merchants, growing impatient at the caravan's delay, began to clamor for their money. They voiced their fears to their friend Ali, who, himself outraged at the cobbler's recklessness, took him aside and spoke to him.

'Have you taken leave of your senses, man?' he exclaimed. 'I told you to toast the bread, not burn it! The merchants are demanding their money and say you owe them sixty thousand pieces of gold. You have squandered all this money among the beggars; how will you ever pay it back, idle as you are, with no work to do or goods to trade with?'

'Never mind,' Maaruf replied. 'What are sixty thousand pieces of gold? When my caravan arrives, if they want gold, they shall have gold; and if they want goods, they shall have goods, for I have vast quantities of them.'

'Now glory be to Allah!' exclaimed his friend. 'What goods are you talking about?'

'Why, the goods in my caravan,' Maaruf replied. 'I have countless bales of merchandise.'

'Dog!' Ali exclaimed. 'Are you telling me that story? Why, I will expose you to the whole world!'

'Away with you!' the cobbler answered. 'Did you suppose I was a poor man? Know, then, I have priceless riches on the way. As soon as my caravan arrives, the merchants will be paid twofold.'

At this Ali grew very angry.

'Scoundrel, I will teach you!' he cried.

'Do your worst!' the cobbler answered. 'They must wait until my caravan arrives; and then they will have their money back and more.'

In despair Ali left Maaruf and went away.

'If I now abuse him after commending him so highly,' he said to himself, 'I shall look like a twofold liar.'

When the merchants returned, inquiring the outcome of his meeting with Maaruf, the harassed Ali said, 'My friends, I had not the heart to speak to him about his debts, for I myself have lent him a thousand pieces. Speak to him yourselves. If he fails to pay you, denounce him to the King as an impostor and a thief.'

The merchants went in a body to the King and told him all that had passed between them and Maaruf.

'Your Majesty,' they said, 'we do not know what to make of this merchant, whose generosity exceeds all bounds. He has borrowed from us sixty thousand pieces of gold, and scattered them in handfuls among the poor. Were he a poor man, he would never be so foolish as to give away so much; and if he is indeed a man of wealth, why has his vaunted caravan not yet arrived?'

Now, the King was an avaricious old miser. When he heard the merchants' account of

Maaruf's extravagance, greed took possession of his soul and he said to his vizier, This man must surely be a merchant of extraordinary wealth, or he would never have been so generous. His caravan is certain to arrive. Now, I will not allow these wolves of the market place to grab all the treasures for themselves, for they are already too rich. I must seek his friendship, so that when his caravan arrives I, too, will have a share. Why, I might even give him my daughter in marriage and join his wealth to mine!'

But the vizier replied, 'The man is an impostor, Your Majesty. Beware of avarice, avarice brings ruin and repentance.'

'I will put him to the test,' said the King, 'and we will soon discover if he is a trickster. I will show him a costly pearl and ask his opinion of it. If he can tell its worth, we will know that he is a rich man accustomed to things of value. If he cannot, we will know that he is a liar and a fraud, and I will put him to a terrible death.'

Maaruf was sent for, and when he had been admitted to the King's presence and had exchanged greetings with him, the King asked, 'Is it true that you owe the merchants sixty thousand pieces of gold?'

Yes, it was true, Maaruf answered. 'Why, then, do you not pay them their money?' asked the King.

'The day my caravan arrives,' came the reply, 'they will be paid twofold. If they want gold, they shall have gold; if they want silver, they shall have silver; and if they prefer goods, they shall have goods, for I have vast quantities of them.'

Then, to test Maaruf, the King handed him a rare pearl worth a thousand gold pieces.

'Have you such pearls in your caravan?' he asked.

Maaruf examined the pearl for a moment and, throwing it disdainfully to the floor, crushed it under his heel.

'What is the meaning of this?' cried the King indignantly.

'This pearl,' replied the cobbler with a laugh, is scarcely worth a thousand pieces of gold. I have vast quantities of much larger pearls in my caravan.'

At this the King's avarice knew no bounds. He sent for the merchants, told them that their fears were groundless, and assured them that the caravan would soon arrive. Then he summoned his minister.

'See that the merchant Maaruf is received with all magnificence at the palace,' he said. 'Speak to him about my daughter, the Princess. Perhaps he will consent to marry her, and so we will gain possession of all his wealth.'

'Your Majesty,' the vizier replied, 'I do not like the manner of this foreigner. His presence bodes evil for the court. I beg you to wait until we have visible proof of his caravan.'

Now, the vizier himself had once sought the Princess' hand in marriage and his suit had been rejected. So when the King heard this warning, he flew into a rage.

'Villain,' he cried, 'you slander this merchant only because you wish to marry the Princess yourself. You would have her left on my hands until she is old and unacceptable. Could she ever find a more suitable husband than this accomplished, wealthy, and generous young man? Not only will he make her a perfect husband, but he will make us all rich into the bargain!'

Afraid of the King's anger, the vizier kept his own counsel and went off to see Maaruf.

'His Majesty the King desires you to marry his daughter, the Princess,' he said. 'What answer shall I give him?'

'I am honored by the King's proposal,' replied Maaruf with an air of unconcern. 'But do you not think it would be better to wait until my caravan arrives? The wedding present for such a bride as the Princess would be a greater expense than I can at present afford. I must give my wife at least five thousand purses of gold. Among the poor of the city I will have to distribute a thousand purses on the bridal night; to those who walk in the wedding procession I must give a thousand more; and I will need another thousand to entertain the troops. On the next morning I must present a hundred precious diamonds to the Princess, and as many jewels to the slave girls of the palace. All this is an expense that cannot be met before my caravan arrives.'

When the vizier returned, the King was so overwhelmed by Maaruf's reply that he invited him at once to a private audience.

'Honored and distinguished merchant,' said the King as soon as the cobbler entered, 'let us celebrate this happy union at once! I myself will meet the expenses of the marriage. My treasury is full; I give you leave to take from it all that you require. You can send in the Princess' present when your caravan arrives. By Allah, I will take no refusal!'

Without a moment's delay the King sent for the Imam of the Royal Mosque, who drew up a marriage contract for Maaruf and the Princess.

The city was gaily decorated on the King's orders. Drums and trumpets sounded in the streets, and Maaruf the cobbler sat enthroned in the great hall of the palace. A troupe of singers, dancers, wrestlers, clowns, and acrobats capered around the court to entertain the guests, while the royal treasurer brought Maaruf bag after bag of gold to scatter among the merry throng. He had no rest that day, for no sooner did he come to Maaruf staggering under the weight of a hundred thousand coins than he was sent back for another load.

The vizier watched this with rage in his heart, while Ali the merchant, aghast at the proceedings, approached Maaruf and whispered in his ear, 'May Allah have no mercy upon you! It is not enough that you have frittered away the wealth of all the merchants? Must you also drain the royal treasury?'

'What's that to you?' replied Maaruf. 'Be sure that when my great caravan arrives, I will repay the King a thousandfold.'

The extravagant rejoicings lasted forty days, and then came the wedding day. The King, accompanied by his ministers and the officers of his army, walked in the bridal procession. Maaruf threw handfuls of gold to the crowds who lined the way.

Next morning he dressed himself in a princely robe and entered the King's council chamber, where he sat down by the side of his father-in-law to receive the good wishes of the ministers and the chief officers of the realm. He sent for the treasurer and ordered him to give robes of honor to all who were present; then he called for sacks of gold and gave handfuls to every member of the royal retinue from the highest courtier to the humblest kitchen boy.

For twenty days Maaruf continued to dissipate the King's treasure. There was still no news of the caravan, and at last came the day when the treasurer found all the coffers empty. He went to tell the King.

'Your Majesty,' he said, 'the treasure chests are empty and the great caravan of your son-in-law has not yet come to fill them.'

Alarmed at these words, the King turned to his vizier.

'By Allah,' he said, 'it is true that there is still no sign of the caravan. What shall we do?'

'Allah prolong your life, my master!' replied the vizier with an evil smile. 'Did I not warn you against the tricks of this impostor? I swear he has no caravan – no, not so much as a one-eyed donkey! He has married your daughter without a present and defrauded you of all your treasure. How long will Your Majesty put up with this rogue?'

'If only we could learn the truth about him!' sighed the King in great perplexity.

'Your Majesty,' said the vizier, 'no one is better able to find out a man's secrets than his wife. I beg you to call your daughter here and permit me to question her from behind a curtain.'

'It shall be done!' the King replied. 'On my life, if it be proved that he has deceived me, he shall die the cruelest of deaths!'

A curtain was drawn across the hall, and the Princess was summoned by the King, who bade her sit behind it and speak with the vizier.

'What do you wish to know?' she asked.

'Honored lady,' began the vizier, 'the chests of the treasury are empty, thanks to the extravagance of Prince Maaruf, but the wondrous caravan, about which we have heard so much, has not yet come. Therefore the King has given me leave to ask what you know of this stranger and whether you have reason to suspect him.'

'Night after night,' replied the Princess, 'he has

promised me pearls and jewels and countless other treasures. But of these I have as yet seen nothing.'

'Your Highness,' said the vizier, 'question him tonight, so that we may know the answer to this riddle. Beg him to tell you the truth, and promise to keep his secret.'

'I hear and obey,' the Princess replied. 'I will speak to Maaruf tonight and tell you what he says.'

In the evening the Princess threw her arms around her husband, saying, 'Light of my eyes, flower of my heart, your love has kindled in me such fires that I would gladly die for you. Tell me the truth about your caravan and hide nothing from me. How long will you fool my father with such lies? For I fear that he will find you out at last and make you pay dearly for this deception. Tell me everything, my love, and I will think of a way to help you.'

'Sweet Princess,' replied Maaruf, 'I will tell you all. I am no wealthy merchant, no master of caravans. In my own land I was a cobbler plagued with a vicious wife called . . .'

And he told the Princess the tale of his misfortunes, from his marriage to his flight to Ikhtiyan-al-Khatan.

When she heard the cobbler's story, the Princess burst into a fit of laughter.

'Truly, Maaruf, you are an extraordinary rogue!' she said. 'But what are we to do? What will my father say when he learns the truth? The vizier has already sown suspicions in his mind. He will surely kill you and I shall die of grief.' She handed him a hundred pieces of gold and said, 'Take these and leave the palace now. Ride away to some far country, and then send a courier to let me know your news.'

'I am at your mercy, mistress,' the cobbler replied.

He said good-by to the Princess and, disguising himself in the livery of a slave, mounted the fastest horse in the King's stables, and rode out into the night.

Next morning, the King sat in the council chamber with the vizier by his side and summoned the Princess to his presence. She came and took her seat behind the curtain as before.

'Tell us, my daughter, what have you learned about Prince Maaruf?'

'May Allah silence all slanderous tongues!' exclaimed the Princess.

'How so?' asked the King.

'Last night,' she went on, 'soon after Maaruf came to my room, the chief of the guards brought in a letter from ten richly dressed slaves who begged to see their master Maaruf. I took the letter and read aloud, "From the five hundred slaves of the caravan to their master the merchant Maaruf. We would have you know that soon after you left us we were attacked by an army of two thousand mounted bedouin. We battled against them for thirty days and thirty nights. The caravan lost fifty of its slaves, a hundred mules, and two hundred loads of merchandise. This is the cause of our delay."

'Yet the Prince was hardly perturbed at this bad news; he did not even ask details from the waiting messengers. "What are two hundred bales and a hundred mules?" he said to me. "At worst the loss cannot be more than seventy thousand pieces of gold. Think no more about it, my dear. One thing alone distresses me, that I shall have to leave you for a few days in order to hasten the arrival of the caravan."

'He got up with a carefree laugh, embraced me tenderly, and said good-by. When he had gone I looked through the window of my room and saw him chatting with ten handsome slaves dressed in uniforms of rare magnificence.

'Presently he mounted his horse and rode away with them to bring the caravan home. Allah be praised that I did not question my husband in the manner you asked,' added the Princess bitterly. 'I would have lost his love and he would have ceased to trust me. It would have been the fault of your hateful vizier, whose only object is to revile my husband and discredit him in your eyes.'

The King rejoiced at these words and exclaimed, 'May Allah increase your husband's wealth and prolong his life, my daughter!' Then, turning to the vizier, he rebuked him angrily and told him henceforth to hold his tongue.

So much for the King, the vizier, and the Princess.

As for Maaruf, sadly he rode far into the desert until he came at midday to the outskirts of a little village. By this time he was tired and very hungry. Seeing an old plowman driving two oxen in a field, he went up him and greeted him. 'Peace be with you,' he said.

The peasant returned his greeting and, noticing the stranger's garb, inquired, 'Doubtless, my master, you are one of the King's servants?'

When Maaruf replied that he was, the plowman welcomed him. 'Dismount and be my guest,' he said.

The cobbler thanked the poor peasant and politely declined his invitation. But the kind old man would take no refusal.

'Pray dismount,' he insisted, 'and grant me the honor of entertaining you. I will go now to the village and bring food for you and hay for your horse.'

'Since the village is near, my friend,' protested Maaruf, 'I can easily ride there myself and buy food in the market.'

But the peasant smiled and shook his head. 'I am afraid you will find no market in a poor hamlet such as ours,' he replied. 'I beg you, in Allah's name, to rest here with your horse while I quickly run to the village.'

Not wishing to offend the peasant, Maaruf dismounted and sat down on the grass, while his host hurried away.

As he waited for the peasant's return, Maaruf

thought, 'I am keeping this poor man from his work. I will make up for his lost time by working at the plow myself.'

He went up to the oxen and drove the plow along the furrow. The beasts had not gone far, however, when the plowshare struck against an object in the ground and came to a sudden halt. Maaruf goaded the oxen on, but though they strained powerfully against the yoke, the plow remained rooted in the ground. Clearing away the soil, Maaruf found that the share had caught in a great ring of gold set in a marble slab the size of a large millstone. He moved the slab aside and saw below it a flight of stairs. Going down the stairs, he found himself in a square vault as large as a city's baths, with four separate halls. The first was filled with gold from floor to ceiling; the second, with pearls, emeralds, and coral; the third, with rubies and turquoises; and the fourth, with diamonds and other precious stones. At the far side of the vault stood a coffer of clearest crystal, and upon it a golden casket no larger than a lemon.

The cobbler marveled and rejoiced at this discovery. He went up to the little casket and, lifting the lid, found in it a gold signet ring finely engraved with strange inscriptions that resembled the legs of creeping insects. He slipped the ring upon his finger and, in doing so, rubbed the seal.

At once a mighty jinnee appeared before him, saying, 'I am here, master, I am here! Speak and I will obey. What is your wish? Would you have me build a capital, or lay a town in ruins? Would you have me slay a king, or dig a river bed? I am your slave, by order of the Sovereign of the World, Creator of the day and night! What is your wish?'

Maaruf was amazed at the apparition.

'Who are you?' he cried.

'I am the slave of the ring,' the jinnee answered. 'Faithfully I serve my master, and my master is he who rubs the ring. Nothing is beyond my power; for I am lord over seventy-two tribes of jinn, each two and seventy thousand strong. Each jinnee rules over a thousand giants, each giant over a thousand goblins, each goblin over a thousand demons, and each demon over a thousand imps. All these owe me absolute allegiance; and yet, for all my power, I have no choice but to obey my master. Ask what you will, and it shall be done. Be it on land or sea, by day or night, should you need me you have but to rub the ring, and I will be at hand to carry out your orders. Of one thing only I must warn you: if you rub the ring twice, I will be consumed in the fire of the powerful words engraved on the seal, and you will lose me for ever.'

'Slave of the ring,' said Maaruf, 'can you tell me what this place is and who imprisoned you in this ring?'

'The vault in which you stand, my master,' replied the jinnee, 'is the ancient treasure house of Shaddad Ibn Aad, King of Iram. While he lived I was his servant and dwelt in this ring. Just before his death he locked it away in this treasure house, and it was your good fortune to find it.'

'Slave of the ring,' said the cobbler, 'can you carry all this treasure to the open?'

'That is very easy,' the jinnee replied.

'Then do so without delay,' said Maaruf, 'and leave nothing in this vault.'

Scarcely had he uttered these words when the floor opened and there appeared before him several handsome boys with baskets upon their heads. These they quickly filled with gold and jewels and carried them above ground. In a few moments the four halls were emptied of their treasure.

'Who are these boys?' Maaruf asked.

'They are my own sons,' the jinnee replied. 'A light task such as this does not require the mustering of a mighty band. What else do you wish, my master?'

'I require a caravan of mules loaded with chests,' replied the cobbler, 'to carry these marvels to Ikhtiyan-al-Khatan.'

The jinnee uttered a loud cry, and there appeared seven hundred richly saddled mules laden with chests and baskets, and a hundred slaves magnificently clad. In a twinkling the chests and baskets were filled with treasure and placed upon the mules, and the caravan stood in splendid array, guarded by mounted slaves.

'And now, slave of the ring,' said Maaruf, 'I require a few hundred loads of precious stuffs.'

'Would you have Syrian damask or Persian velvet, Indian brocade or Roman silk or Egyptian gabardine?'

'A hundred loads of each!' cried Maaruf.

'I hear and obey,' replied the jinnee. 'I will at once dispatch my spirits to these distant lands. Tomorrow morning you shall have all that you require.'

Then Maaruf ordered the slave of the ring to set up a pavilion and serve him food and wine. The jinnee provided his master with a silk pavilion and a sumptuous meal and departed on his mission.

As Maaruf was about to sit down to his feast, the old peasant returned from the village, carrying a large bowl of lentils for his guest and a sack of hay for the horse. When he saw the great caravan drawn up in the field, and Maaruf reclining in the tent, attended by innumerable slaves, he thought that his guest must be none other than the King.

'I will hurry back,' he said to himself, 'and kill my two chickens and roast them in butter for him.' He was on the point of turning back when Maaruf saw him and ordered his slaves to bring him into the pavilion.

The slaves led the plowman to the tent, with his bowl of lentils and his sack of hay. Maaruf rose to receive him and gave him a courteous welcome.

'What is it you are carrying, brother?' he asked.

'Master,' the peasant replied. 'I was bringing you your dinner and some hay for your horse. Pardon my scant courtesy, I beg you. Had I known you were the King, I would have killed my two chickens and roasted them for you.'

'Do not be alarmed, my friend,' replied Maaruf. 'I am not the King, but his son-in-law. A certain misunderstanding arose between us and I left the palace. I will return tomorrow morning with these messengers and these presents.'

Then Maaruf thanked the peasant for his generosity and made him sit down by his side. 'By Allah,' he said, 'I will eat nothing but the food of your hospitality.'

He ordered the slaves to serve the peasant with the delicate meats and ate the lentils himself. When the meal was finished he filled the empty bowl with gold and gave it to the peasant.

'Take this to your family,' he said, 'and if you come to see me at the palace you will have a hearty welcome and a generous reward.'

The old plowman took the gold and returned to the village, scarcely believing his good fortune.

When darkness fell, the slaves of the caravan brought into the tent a troupe of beautiful girls, who danced and made music. At daybreak Maaruf saw a great cloud of dust in the distance, and soon a long procession of mules drew near. They were laden with innumerable bales of merchandise, and at their head rode the jinnee, in the guise of a caravan leader, alongside a four-pillared litter of pure gold inlaid with diamonds. When the caravan arrived at the tent, the jinnee dismounted and kissed the ground before Maaruf.

'The task is accomplished, my master,' he said. 'Pray put on the garment that I have brought especially for you; you will find it worthy of a king. Then mount this litter.'

'One thing more remains to be done,' said Maaruf. 'Before I set forth with the caravan, I wish you to hurry to Ikhtiyan-al-Khatan and announce my coming to the King.'

'I hear and obey,' the jinnee replied.

He transformed himself into the semblance of a courier and set off toward the city, arriving at the palace just as the vizier was saying to the King, 'Be no longer deceived, Your Majesty, by the lies of this impostor. Do not be taken in by your daughter's story; for I swear by your precious life that Maaruf fled the city, not to speed the arrival of his caravan, but to save his skin.'

As the vizier finished speaking, the courier entered the royal presence and kissed the ground before the King.

'Your Majesty,' he said, 'I bring you greetings from the illustrious Prince, your son-in-law, who is now approaching the city with his noble caravan.'

With this the courier again kissed the ground before the King and hurried out of the palace. The King rejoiced. 'Traitor,' he said to the vizier, 'may Allah blacken your face. How long will you revile my son-in-law and call him thief and liar?'

The dumbfounded vizier hung his head.

The city was decorated, and a procession marched out to meet the caravan. The King went to his daughter's room and told her the joyful news. The Princess was astounded to hear her father speak of the caravan and thought, 'Can this be another of Maaruf's tricks? Or was he testing my love with an invented tale of poverty?'

But even more astonished than the Princess was her husband's friend, Ali the merchant. When he saw the great commotion in the city and learned the news of Maaruf's expected arrival at the head of a splendid caravan, he thought, 'What new roguery is this? Can it be possible that this patcher of old slippers is really coming with a caravan? Or is it some fresh trick he has contrived with the aid of the Princess?'

Before long, the procession that had gone out to meet the caravan returned to the city. Maaruf, arrayed in a magnificent robe, rode triumphantly by the King's side in the golden litter, and as the long, winding caravan made its way through the streets, the merchants flocked near their prodigal debtor and kissed the ground before him. Ali the merchant managed to push his way through the throng and whispered to Maaruf, 'How on earth has this come about, you sheikh of mad swindlers? And yet, by Allah, you deserve your good fortune!'

The procession halted at the royal palace. In the great council chamber, Maaruf sat beside the King. He ordered his slaves to fill the royal coffers with gold and jewels, and to unpack the bales of precious merchandise. Then he picked out the finest stuffs and said to the attendants, 'Carry these silks to the Princess so that she may distribute them among her women; also take her this chest of jewels, which she may share among the slaves and serving girls.'

After that he proceeded to deal out presents to the officers of the King's army, to the courtiers and their wives, to the merchants who were his creditors, and to the poor of the city; and while the treasures were being distributed, the King writhed upon his throne in an agony of greed and envy. As Maaruf threw handfuls of pearls and emeralds to right and left, the King whispered to him, 'Enough, my son! There will be nothing left for us!' But Maaruf answered, 'My caravan is inexhaustible.'

It was not long before the vizier came and told the King that the treasury was full and could hold no more. The King cried, 'Fill another hall!'

Then Maaruf hastened to his wife, who received him in a transport of joy and kissed his hand.

'Was it to mock me,' she said, 'or to test my love that you pretended to be a poor cobbler fleeing from a nagging wife? Whichever it was, I thank Allah I did not fail you.'

Maaruf embraced her and gave her a gown splendidly embroidered in gold, a necklace threaded with forty pearls, and a pair of anklets fashioned by the art of mighty sorcerers. The Princess cried out for joy as she saw these marvels, and said, 'I will keep them for festivals and state occasions only.'

'Not so, my love,' replied Maaruf. 'I will give you ornaments like these each day.'

Then he summoned the slave girls of the harem and gave each of them an embroidered robe adorned with ornaments of gold. Arrayed in this splendor, they were like black-eyed maidens of paradise, while the Princess shone in their midst like the moon among the stars.

At nightfall the King said to the vizier, 'What have you to say now? Does not the wealth of my son-in-law surpass all wonders?'

'Indeed, Your Majesty,' the vizier replied, 'the Prince's lavishness is that of no ordinary merchant; for where can a merchant find such pearls and jewels as your son-in-law has thrown away? Kings and princes have no treasures like these. There must surely be some strange reason for his conduct. I suggest, my master, that you make Prince Maaruf drunk if you wish to discover the source of his riches. When he is overcome with wine, let us ply him with questions until he tells us everything. Indeed, I already fear the consequences of this extraordinary wealth; for it is more than likely that in time he will win over the troops with his favors and drive you from your kingdom.'

'You have spoken wisely, my vizier,' said the King. 'Tomorrow we must find out the whole truth.'

Next morning, while the King was sitting in his council chamber, the grooms of the royal stables rushed in, begging leave to speak with him.

'Your Majesty,' they cried, 'the entire caravan of Prince Maaruf is gone! All the slaves, the horses, and the mules disappeared during the night, and nowhere can we find a trace of them.'

Greatly troubled at this news, the King hastened to Maaruf's chamber and told him what had happened. But Maaruf laughed.

'Calm yourself, Your Majesty,' he said. 'The loss of these trifles is nothing to me. For what is a caravan of mules?'

'By Allah,' thought the King in amazement, 'what manner of man is this, to whom wealth counts for nothing? There must surely be a reason for all this!'

When evening came, the King sat with Maaruf and the vizier in a pavilion in the garden of the palace. Wine flowed freely; and when Maaruf was so flushed with drink that he could not tell his left hand from his right, the vizier said to him, 'Your Highness, you have never told us the adventures of your life. Pray let us hear how you became so rich and rose to such prominence in business affairs.'

Thereupon the drunken cobbler related the story of his life, from his marriage in Cairo to the finding of the ring in the peasant's field.

'Will you permit us to see the ring, Your Highness?' asked the vizier.

Without a moment's thought the foolish cobbler slipped the ring from his finger and handed it to the minister.

'Look at the seal!' he said. 'My servant the jinnee dwells within it.'

The vizier instantly slipped the ring upon his own finger and rubbed the seal; and the jinnee appeared before him.

'I am here,' said the jinnee. 'Ask and receive! Would you have me build a capital, or lay a town in ruins? Would you have me slay a king, or dig a river bed?'

'Slave of the ring,' replied the vizier, pointing to Maaruf, 'take up this rascal and cast him down upon some barren desert where he will perish from hunger and thirst!'

At once the jinnee snatched up the cobbler, flew with him between earth and sky, and finally set him down in the middle of a waterless desert.

'Did I not tell you,' said the vizier to the King, 'that this dog was a liar and a cheat?'

'You were right, my vizier,' replied the monarch. 'Give me the ring and let me examine it.'

'Miserable old fool,' the vizier cried, 'do you expect me to remain your servant when I can be your master?'

So saying, the vizier rubbed the ring and said to the jinnee, 'Take up this wretch and cast him down by the side of his son-in-law!'

The jinnee carried the old King upon his shoulder, flew with him through the void, and set him down in the middle of the desert, where King and son-in-law sat wailing together. So much for them.

The vizier summoned the nobles and the captains of the army and proclaimed himself Sultan of the city. He explained that he had banished the King and Maaruf by the power of a magic ring, and threatened the assembly, saying, 'If anyone dares to resist my rule, he shall join them in the desert of hunger and thirst!'

The courtiers swore fealty, and the vizier promoted some and dismissed others. Then he sent a message to the Princess, bidding her prepare to receive him that night.

'You will be welcome,' the Princess answered through her footman.

When evening came, she put on her silks and jewels, perfumed herself, and received the vizier with a smile. 'What an honor, my master,' she said, and invited him to sit down.

'Now that we are alone, Your Highness,' said the vizier, 'I pray that you unveil yourself.'

The Princess readily complied, but scarcely had she done so than she uttered a cry of terror and started back, covering her face again.

'What is the matter, my mistress?' asked the vizier.

'Would you show my face to that stranger?' she cried in terror.

'Where, where?' exclaimed the vizier angrily.

'There, in your ring!'

The vizier laughed, and said, 'Dear lady, that is no man but only my faithful jinnee.'

But the Princess screamed louder and cried, 'I am terrified of the jinnee! Put him away, for my sake!'

The vizier took the ring off his finger and placed it under the cushions. Thereupon she gave a loud cry, and at once forty slave girls burst into the room and laid hold of the vizier. The Princess quickly snatched up the ring and rubbed the seal; and the jinnee appeared before her.

'Cast this traitor into a dark dungeon,' she said, 'and bring me back my father and my husband.'

'I hear and obey,' the jinnee replied; and, carrying the vizier on his shoulder, threw him into the darkest dungeon of the palace. Then he flew toward the desert and presently returned with the King and Maaruf, both half dead with fright and hunger.

The Princess, rejoicing to see them, offered them food and wine and told them how she had outwitted the vizier.

'We will tie him to the stake and put him to death!' the King cried. 'But first give me back the ring, my daughter.

The Princess replied, 'The ring shall stay with me. I will take care of it from now on.'

Early next morning the King and Maaruf entered the council chamber. The courtiers, who were astonished to see them, again kissed the ground before them and gave them a jubilant welcome. The stake was set up in the grounds of the palace and the vizier was put to death in sight of all the people.

Maaruf was appointed vizier and heir to the throne. He governed jointly with the King, and lived with the Princess ever after.

THE TALE OF THE HUNCHBACK

Once upon a time, in the city of Basra, a tailor was taking an evening walk with his wife when they met a sprightly little hunchback who was merrily singing and clashing a tambourine. His merriment was so infectious that it banished grief and sorrow and every other care. The couple were so amused by the hunchback that they invited him to spend the evening with them as their guest. He accepted, and when they had reached home the tailor hurried out to the market place, where he bought some fried fish, bread, and lemons, and honey for desert.

The three sat down to a hilarious meal. Being

fond of practical jokes, the tailor's wife crammed a large piece of fish into the hunchback's mouth and forced him to swallow it. But, as fate would have it, the fish concealed a large and sharp bone that stuck in his throat and choked him. When they examined him they found, to their horror, that the hunchback was dead.

The tailor lifted up his hands and exclaimed, 'There is no strength or power save in Allah! Alas that this man should have met his death at our hands, and in this fashion!'

'Crying will not help us,' said his wife. 'We must do something!'

'What can we do?' whimpered the tailor.

'Take the body in your arms,' she said. 'We will cover it with a shawl and carry it out of the house this very night. I will walk in front, crying, "My child is ill, my poor child is ill! Who can direct us to a doctor's house?"'

Encouraged by her plan, the tailor wrapped up the hunchback in a large silken shawl and carried him out into the street, his wife lamenting, 'My child! My child! Who will save him from the foul smallpox?'

So all who saw them whispered, 'They are carrying a child stricken with the smallpox.'

Thus they proceeded through the streets, inquiring for the doctor's house as they went, until at last they were directed to the house of a Jewish doctor. They knocked, and the door was opened by a slave girl.

'Give your master this piece of silver,' said the tailor's wife, 'and beg him to come down and see my child; for he is very ill.'

As soon as the girl had gone in to call the doctor, the tailor's wife slipped into the doorway and said to her husband, 'Let us leave the hunchback here and run for our lives!'

The tailor propped up the body at the bottom of the staircase, and the pair made off as fast as their legs could carry them.

The Jew rejoiced on receiving the piece of silver. He rose quickly and, hurrying down the stairs in the dark, stumbled against the corpse and knocked it over. Terrified at the sight of the lifeless hunchback, and thinking that he himself had just caused his death, the Jew called on Moses and Aaron and Ezra and Joshua son of Nun, and reminded himself of the Ten Commandments, wringing his hands and crying, 'How will I get rid of the body?' Then he took up the hunchback and bore him to his wife and told her what had happened.

'You stand there doing nothing?' exclaimed the terrified woman. 'If the corpse remains here till daybreak we are lost! Come, we will carry the body up to the terrace and throw it into the courtyard of our neighbor the Moslem.'

Now, the Moslem was the steward of the royal kitchens, from which he seldom departed with his pockets empty. His house was always infested with rats and mice, which ate the butter, the cheese, and the wheat; and on fine nights the stray cats and dogs of the neighborhood came down and feasted on the contents of the kitchen. So the Jew and his wife, carrying the hunchback, climbed down from their terrace into their neighbor's courtyard and propped the hunchback up against the wall of the kitchen.

It was not long before the steward, who had been out all day, returned home. He opened the door and lit a candle – then started at the sight of a man leaning against the wall of his kitchen. 'So our thief is a man after all!' he thought; and, taking up a mallet, he cried, 'By Allah! to think it was you, and not the cats and dogs, who stole the meat and the butter! I have killed almost all the stray cats and dogs of the district and never thought of you and your like, who come prowling around the terraces.'

He knocked the hunchback down with the mallet and dealt him another blow on the chest as he lay on the ground. But the angry steward soon found that the man was dead. He was seized with fear, and exclaimed, 'There is no strength or power save in Allah! A curse upon the meat and the butter, and upon this night which has witnessed your death at my hands, you wretch!'

He lifted the hunchback onto his shoulders and left the house. The night was already nearing its end. The steward walked with his burden through the deserted streets until he entered a lane leading to the market place, and came to a shop that stood on a corner. There he leaned the hunchback up against the wall and hurried away.

Soon after, a Christian, who was the king's saddler, passed through the lane on his way to the public baths. He was fuddled with drink, and as he reeled along, he kept muttering to himself, 'Doomsday has come! The Last Judgment has come!' and staggering from one side of the lane to the other. Suddenly he bumped into the hunchback.

Now, it so chanced that earlier in the evening the Christian had been robbed of his turban and was forced to buy another. So, on suddenly seeing this figure against the wall, he imagined, in his stupor, that it was someone who was about to snatch off his new turban and, taking the hunchback by the throat, felled him with a resounding blow. Then he raised a great outcry, screaming and cursing and calling out to the watchman of the market place.

The watchman arrived to find a Christian beating a Moslem.

'Get up and let go of him!' he shouted angrily Then he found that the hunchback was dead. 'A fine state of affairs when a Christian dares to kill a Believer!' he exclaimed.

Confounded at the swift death of his victim, the Christian began to call on Jesus and Mary: thus, as the proverb has it, intoxication departed and meditation took its place. The watchman took hold of the Christian saddler, manacled him, and dragged him away to the governor's house.

In the morning the governor gave orders for the hanging of the Christian. The town crier proclaimed his crime in the streets, and a gallows was set up in the heart of the city. Then came the executioner who, in the presence of the governor, stood the Christian beneath the gallows and put the rope around his neck.

At this moment the King's steward pushed his way through the crowd, crying, 'Do not hang him! It was I who killed the hunchback!'

'Why did you kill him?' asked the governor.

'It all happened,' replied the steward, 'when I returned home last night and found him in my house, about to break into the kitchen. I struck him with a mallet and he fell down dead upon the instant. In despair, I carried him to a lane adjoining the market place. Is it not enough to have killed a Moslem?' added the steward passionately. 'Must a Christian also die on my account? Therefore, hang no man but me!'

Hearing this, the governor set the Christian free and gave the executioner a fresh order. 'Hang the steward instead, on the grounds of his own confession.'

The executioner led the steward to the scaffold and had just placed the rope around his neck when the Jewish doctor forced his way through the crowd. 'Do not hang him!' he cried. 'I am the man who killed the hunchback!' And he told the governor his own version of the hunchback's death. 'Is my sin not great enough that I have killed a man unwittingly?' he added. 'Must another be killed through my crime, and with my knowledge?'

On hearing this, the governor gave orders that the Jew be hanged in place of the steward. But as the rope was being placed around his neck, the tailor came forward and cried, 'Do not hang him! No one killed the hunchback but myself!' And he related to the astonished assembly the true circumstances of the hunchback's death.

The governor marveled at the story and commented, 'This episode ought to be recorded in books.' And he ordered the executioner to set the Jew at liberty and to hang the tailor.

'Would to heaven they would make up their minds,' muttered the executioner, understandably impatient at the delay. 'The day will end before we hang any of them.' He resolutely placed the rope around the tailor's neck.

Now, the hunchback, the cause of all this commotion, was the King's jester and favorite companion. Finding that his jester had been absent from the royal palace all night and all the next morning, the monarch ordered his attendants to look for him. They soon returned to inform him of the hunchback's death and his self-confessed murderers.

'Go to the governor,' said the King to his chamberlain, 'and get him to bring them all before me.'

The chamberlain hurried at once to the city square, where the executioner was about to hang the tailor. 'Stop! Stop! Don't hang him!' he shouted, rushing through the crowd. And before the executioner could complete his work, the chamberlain informed the governor of the King's orders and took him to the royal palace, together with the tailor, the Christian, the Jew, the steward, and the hunchback's body.

When they had all been admitted to the King's presence, the governor kissed the ground before him and related all that had happened. The King marveled greatly and gave orders that the story be inscribed on parchment in letters of gold. Then he turned to those who were present and asked, 'Have you ever heard a tale more astonishing than this story of the hunchback?'

The tailor came forward, and said, 'Of all the tales of marvel that I have heard, Your Majesty, none surpasses in wonder an incident that I witnessed yesterday.

'Early in the morning, before I met the hunchback, I was at a breakfast party given by a friend to some twenty tradesmen and craftsmen of the city, among them tailors, drapers, carpenters, and others. As soon as the sun rose and the food was set before us, our host ushered into the room a handsome but noticeably lame young man, richly dressed in the Baghdad fashion. The young man greeted the company, and we all rose to receive him. But when he was about to sit down, he caught sight of one of the guests and, instead of taking his seat, made for the door. We all expressed surprise and concern, and our host held the young man by the arm and earnestly pleaded with him to explain his abrupt departure.

'"Sir," he answered, "do not try to detain me. If you must know, it is the presence of this obnoxious barber that compels me to leave at once."

'Our host was greatly astonished at these words, and the rest of us, too, wondered why the young man, a stranger in this city, should have taken offense at the barber's presence. We begged him to tell us the reason.

'"Gentlemen," he answered, "this barber was the cause of a grave disaster that befell me in Baghdad, my native city. Thanks to him my leg was broken and I am now lame. I have sworn never to sit in the same room with him, nor live in any town where he resides. This is why I left Baghdad, yet here I find him again. Not another night will I spend in this city."

'"By Allah," we said, "let us hear your story."

'The barber hung his head as the young man proceeded to tell of his adventure.'

The Tale of the Lame Young Man and the Barber of Baghdad

You should know that my father was one of the chief merchants of Baghdad and I was his only son. When I reached manhood my father died, leaving me great wealth and a numerous retinue of slaves and servants. From that time I began to live sumptuously, wearing the richest clothes and eating the choicest dishes. But I always avoided the company of women, for I felt shy and uneasy with them.

It so chanced, however, that one day, as I was walking along a narrow lane in Baghdad, a crowd of women barred my way. To get away from them

I slipped into a quiet alleyway and sat down on a bench. I had not been there long when a window in the house opposite was flung open, and there appeared a young girl who was like the full moon in her beauty. She was watering the flowerpots on her window sill when, glancing around for the moment, she caught sight of me; whereupon she shut the window and disappeared. I fell in love with her at first sight and sat there forgetful of my surroundings until sunset, when the cadi of Baghdad came riding by, with slaves before him and servants behind him. Imagine my feelings, gentlemen, when I saw him dismount and enter the very house where the young girl lived; for I then realized that she was the cadi's daughter.

I returned home very sad at the thought that I would never be able to make her acquaintance. Presently, however, there entered my room an old woman of my household, who at once understood the cause of my sadness. She sat at my bedside and comforted me, saying, 'Tell me everything, my son, and let me be your messenger.'

When she had heard my story she said, 'You must know that this girl lives with her father, the cadi, in the strictest seclusion. But I am a frequent visitor to their house, and I will undertake to bring you together. Do not despair. I will go there at once.'

I was greatly consoled by her words. The old woman departed on her errand but soon returned crestfallen.

'My son,' she said, 'do not ask the outcome of my visit. Scarcely had I begun to speak of you when the girl cried, "Hold your tongue, old woman, or you will receive the punishment you deserve."'

Seeing that this news had dashed my spirits, the old woman added, 'Do not fear – I will shortly approach her again.'

My grief was almost too deep to bear until, after a few days, the woman came again and said, 'Rejoice, I bring you good news! Yesterday I visited the girl again. When she saw me in tears and asked me the reason for my weeping, I replied, "I have come from a young man who is languishing with love for you." Her heart was moved, and she asked, "Who may he be?" "He is the flower of my life," I answered, "and as dear to me as my own son. Some days ago he saw you at your window, watering your flowers. He loved you from that moment. But when I told him of your harsh response after I mentioned him to you, he began to pine away and took to his bed, where he now lies dying." "And all this on account of me?" asked the girl, moved with pity and love. "Yes, by Allah," I replied. "Go back to him," she said. "Give him my greetings and say that my love is as great as his. Ask him to come and see me on Friday next, before the midday prayers. I will let him into the house myself. But he must leave before my father returns from the mosque."'

This report filled me with joy and I handsomely

rewarded the old woman for her labors. My grief completely left me, and my household rejoiced at my recovery.

When Friday came, I made ready for the great occasion, putting on my finest robes and sweetest perfumes, and then sat waiting for the hour of midday prayers. But the old woman hinted that a visit from the barber might do much to improve my appearance. I called my slave and said to him, 'Go to the market place and bring me a barber. See that he is a man of sense who will attend to his business and will not annoy me with idle chatter.' The slave went away and brought back with him a barber who was none other than the odious old man you see before you.

As soon as he arrived, the barber said that I looked very pale; and when I explained that I had but recently recovered from an illness, he congratulated me, saying, 'May Allah preserve you, sir, from all misfortune, all distress, all grief, and all sorrow!'

'Allah grant your prayer!' I replied.

'Now tell me, sir,' he said, 'do you wish to have your head shaved? You doubtless know that the famous Ibn Abbas (may Allah rest his soul in peace!) has said, "He who has his head shaved on a Friday will ward off seventy calamities."'

'Enough of this talk, old man!' I cried. 'Come now, begin shaving my head at once.'

He produced from his pocket a large bundle. Imagine my astonishment when I saw him take from it, not a razor or a pair of scissors as one might have expected, but an astrological device made of seven plates of polished silver. He carried it to the middle of the courtyard, and, raising the instrument toward the sun, gazed intently at the reflection for a long time. Then he came back to me and said solemnly, 'Know that of this day, Friday the tenth of the second month of the year two hundred and fifty-three after the Flight of the Prophet (upon whom be Allah's blessing and peace), and twelve hundred and thirty-one in the year of Alexander the Great, there have elapsed eight degrees and six minutes; and that, according to the strictest rules of computation, the planet Mars, in conjunction with Mercury, is this day in the ascendant: all this denoting an excellent moment for haircutting. Furthermore, my instrument clearly informs me that it is your intention to pay a visit to a certain person, and that of this nothing shall come but evil. There is also another sign in connection with a certain matter, of which I would rather not speak.'

'By Allah!' I cried, 'this is intolerable! You weary me with your tedious chatter, and, what is more, your forebodings are far from encouraging. I sent for you to shave my head. Do so at once and cease your babbling!'

'If only you knew the gravity of the impending disaster,' he said, 'you would listen to my advice and heed the warning of the stars!'

'Doubtless,' I cried, 'you are the only astrologer among the barbers of Baghdad: but, allow me to tell you, old man, you are also an impudent mischief-maker and a frivolous chatterbox.'

'What would you have?' cried he, shrugging his shoulders. 'Allah has sent you one who is not only a barber of great repute, but also a master of the arts and sciences: one who is not only deeply versed in alchemy, astrology, mathematics, and architecture, but also (to mention only a few of my accomplishments) well taught in the arts of logic, rhetoric, and elocution. Add to all this the maturity of judgment that can be acquired only through long experience of the world. Your late father, young man, loved me for my wisdom; and it is the memory of his goodness and kind favors that prompts me to render you an honest service. Far from being a meddlesome gossip, as you seem to suggest, I am, in fact, well known for my gravity and reserve; on account of which qualities people call me 'the Silent One.' Instead of crossing and thwarting me, young man, it would be much more befitting to thank Allah for my sound advice and my concern for your well-being. Would that I were a whole year in your service, that you might learn to do me justice!'

Here I exclaimed, 'You will surely be my death this day!' But when the old man was about to resume his talk, I felt as though I were about to explode with rage, so I said to my slave, 'In

Allah's name, give this man a silver piece and show him out, for I do not wish to have my head shaved after all.'

'What kind of talk is this?' cried the barber. 'By Allah, I will accept nothing before I have shaved you. You must know that I would regard it as a pleasant duty and a great honor to serve you even without payment. For although you do not seem to appreciate my merits, I appreciate yours. I remember one Friday when I was sent for by your late father (may Allah have mercy upon him: he was a man of rare qualities). I found him entertaining a company of visitors. He welcomed me as he might have welcomed an old friend, and said, 'I beg you to cut my hair.' At once I took out my astrolabe, computed the height of the sun, and soon ascertained that the hour was clearly unfavorable for haircutting. I did not hesitate to tell him the truth. He accepted my judgment and readily agreed to wait for a good moment. Incidentally, it might interest you to know that, while we waited, I composed half a dozen verses in his praise and recited them before the company. Your father was so pleased with them that he ordered his slave to give me a hundred and three dinars and a robe of honor. When the awaited hour had come and I had cut his hair, I asked him in a whisper, "Why did you pay me a hundred and three dinars?" "One dinar is for your wisdom," he replied, "one for the hair-cutting, and one for the pleasure of your company; as for the remainder and the robe of honor, pray accept them as a slight reward for your excellent poem." '

'Then may Allah have mercy on my father,' I burst out, 'if he ever had dealings with a barber like you!'

'There is no god but Allah, and Mohammed is his Prophet!' exclaimed the barber, laughing and shaking his head. 'Glory to him who changes others and remains himself unchanged! I always took you for a sensible and intelligent young man: now I see that your illness has slightly affected your head. You would do well to remember that Allah in his Sacred Book mentioned with special praise those who curb their anger and forgive their fellow men. I will forgive you.

'As I was saying, neither your father nor your grandfather before him ever did anything without first seeking my advice. You have doubtless heard the proverb "He who takes good counsel is crowned with success." Now, you will find no one better versed in the ways of the world than myself; and here I stand, waiting to serve you. What I cannot understand, however, is that you seem to be a little tired of me, when I am not in the least tired of you. But the high esteem in which I hold your father's memory will always make me mindful of my duty to his son.'

'By Allah,' I yelled, 'this has gone too far!' I was about to order my slaves to throw him out of the house when he suddenly began to dampen my hair, and before I knew what was happening my head was covered with lather.

'I will take no offense, sir,' continued the wretched old man, quite unruffled, 'if you are a little short-tempered. Apart from the strain of your recent illness, you are, of course, very young. It seems but yesterday that I used to carry you to school on my shoulders.'

Unable to contain myself any longer, I said solemnly, 'My friend, I must beg you to get on with your work.'

'And have I, sir, all this time, been engaged in anything else?' was his reply.

Here I tore my clothes and began to shriek like a madman.

When he saw me do this, the barber calmly produced a razor and began to strop it, passing it up and down the piece of leather with deadly deliberation. At length, he held my head with one hand and shaved off a few hairs. Then he raised his hand and said, 'I do not suppose you are aware of my standing in society. These hands of mine have dressed the heads of kings and princes, viziers and noblemen. Have you not heard the poet's verses in my praise?'

At this point I interrupted him again. 'You have stifled me with your nonsense!'

'It has just occurred to me that you might be in a hurry,' said the barber.

'I am,' I shouted, 'I am!'

'Well, well,' he went on, 'haste is a bad thing

and leads only to ruin and repentance. The Prophet said: "The best enterprises are those that are carried out with caution." I wish you would tell me the purpose of your haste, as there are yet quite three hours to midday prayers.' Here the barber paused, and then added, 'But let me first make sure of the correct time.'

So saying, he flung away the razor, took up the astrolabe, and went out into the courtyard. There he observed the sun for a long time, and at last came back, saying, 'It is now three hours to midday prayers, neither one minute more nor one minute less.'

'For Allah's sake,' I cried, 'hold your tongue! You have goaded me beyond endurance.'

Again he took up the razor and proceeded to strop it as he had done before. Scarcely had he removed a few hairs when he again stopped and said, 'I am rather anxious about you, you know. It would be in your own interest to tell me the cause of your haste. For, as you know, your father and grandfather never did anything without consulting me.'

I realized that I should never be able to evade his persistent questioning. To cut the matter short, I said that I had been invited to a party at the house of a friend and begged him to stop being impertinent.

At the mention of a party the barber exclaimed, 'This reminds me that I myself am expecting a few friends at my house today. But I have forgotten to provide anything for them to eat. Think of the disgrace!'

'Do not be troubled over this matter,' I replied. 'All the food and drink in my house is yours if you will only finish shaving my head.'

'Sir,' he cried, 'may Allah reward you for your generosity! Pray let me hear what you have for my guests.'

'Five different meat dishes,' I answered, 'ten stuffed chickens finely broiled, and a roasted lamb!'

'Be so good,' he said, 'as to let me look at them.'

I ordered the provisions to be brought before him, together with a cask of wine.

'How generous you are!' he exclaimed. 'But what shall we do without incense and perfume?'

I ordered my slave to set before him a box containing aloeswood, musk, and ambergris, the whole worth not less than fifty gold pieces. Time was running short, so I said, 'All this is yours; only, for the sake of Mohammed, on whom be Allah's blessing and peace, finish shaving my head!'

'Pray allow me to see the contents of the box,' he replied.

My slave opened it, and the barber put aside his razor and sat down on the floor, examining the incense. He then rose and, taking up his razor again, held my head and shaved off a few more hairs.

'My son,' he said, with great satisfaction, 'I do not know how to thank you. The party I am giving today will now owe a great deal to your kindness. Although none of my guests might be considered worthy of such magnificence, they are all quite respectable. First, there is Zantoot, the bathkeeper; then Salee'a, the corn merchant; Akrasha, the fruit seller; Hamid, the trash collector; Silat, the grocer; Abu Makarish, the milkman; Kaseem, the watchman; and last, but by no means least, Sa'eed, the camel driver. Each one of them is a delightful companion and has a song and dance of his own invention; and is, like your humble servant, neither inquisitive nor given to idle talk. In truth, no description of my friends can do them justice. If, therefore, you would care to honor us with your company, you will have a more pleasant time, and we will all be the happier. In my opinion, one reason why you would do well not to visit those friends of yours is the possibility of meeting some busybody who will split your head with incessant chatter.'

I choked with rage, and burst into a fit of hysterical laughter, but calmed down sufficiently to say, 'I should be delighted to come some other time. Shave my head now and let me go my way. Besides, your friends must be waiting for you.

'But how I long to introduce you to these excellent fellows!' he continued. 'Once you meet them, you will give up all your friends forever.'

'May Allah give you joy in them,' I said. 'I shall doubtless have the pleasure of meeting them one day.'

'Well, well,' he went on, shrugging his shoulders, 'if you must go to your friends, I will now carry to my guests the presents with which you have favored me. As I do not stand upon ceremony with them I will return without delay to accompany you to your party.'

Here I lost all control of myself and cried, 'There is no strength or help save in Allah! Pray go to your friends and delight your heart with them, and let me go to mine; for they are waiting for me.'

But the barber cried, 'I will not let you go alone.'

'The truth is,' I said, 'that no one may be admitted to the house where I am going except myself.'

'Aha!' he exclaimed. 'It must be a woman, then, or else you would allow me to accompany you. Yet I am the right man for that kind of adventure and could do much in an emergency. Why, you may even get yourself murdered! Furthermore, you know how ruthless the governor is about such secret meetings, particularly on a Friday.'

'Vile old man,' I cried, 'how can you speak so to my face?'

'Did you imagine,' retorted the barber, 'that you could hide such a design from me? My only concern, young man, is to serve you.'

Afraid that my servants might hear the barber's remarks, I made no answer.

The hour of prayer had come and the imams

had already begun their sermons, when at long last the barber finished shaving my head.

'Take away this food to your house,' I said, 'and when you return we will go together to the party.'

But he would not believe my words. 'You want to get rid of me and go alone,' he replied. 'Think of the trap that may have been set for you! By Allah, you shall not leave the house until I come back to accompany you and watch over your safety.'

'Very well,' I said, 'but you must not be late.'

The barber took all the meat and drink I had given him and left me in peace. But if you think the wretch carried the things home, you are wrong. He hired a porter for the task and hid himself in one of the neighboring alleyways.

The muezzins had now intoned their blessings on the Prophet from the minarets of the city. I rose quickly, flung on my cloak, and ran as fast as I could to the girl's house. Finding the door open, I hurried up the stairs to her apartment. But I had scarcely reached the second story when the cadi arrived. Seized by a great fear, I rushed to one of the windows overlooking the alleyway, and was confounded to see the barber (Allah's curse be upon him!) sitting on the doorstep.

Now, it so happened that immediately on his return from the mosque the cadi took it into his head to beat one of his maidservants. She raised an uproar of wailing and screaming. A slave went to her aid, but the furious cadi fell upon him also, and he joined in yelling for help.

Imagining that it was I who was the victim, the barber set up a great outcry in the street, tearing his clothes and scattering dust upon his head. 'Help! Help!' he cried. 'My master is being murdered by the cadi!'

Then, running frantically to my house with a great crowd following him, he roused my people and my servants; and before I knew what was happening they all came, men and women, to the cadi's house, with torn clothes and loosed tresses, lamenting, 'Alas! Our master is dead!'

The clamor in the street was heard by the cadi, who ordered a slave to find out what had happened. The slave quickly returned saying, 'There is a great multitude of men and women at the door. They are all shaking their fists and shouting, "Our master has been murdered!"'

The cadi rose in anger and opened the door to find an infuriated mob shouting threats at him.

'What is the meaning of this?' he demanded indignantly.

'Dog! Pig! Murderer!' shouted my servants. 'Where is our master?'

'What has your master done to me,' asked the cadi, 'that I should kill him?'

'You have just been flogging him,' replied the barber. 'I myself heard his cries.'

'But what has your master done that I should

flog him?' repeated the cadi. 'And who brought him to my house?'

'Wicked old liar,' answered the barber, 'do not pretend to be so innocent, for I know the whole truth and every detail of the matter. Your daughter is in love with him and he with her. When you caught him in the house you ordered your slaves to flog him. By Allah, the Caliph himself shall judge this outrage! Give us back our master, or else I will have to enter by force and rescue him myself.'

Embarrassed and perplexed, the cadi said, 'If you are not lying, come and bring him out.'

I saw the barber push his way through the door. I desperately looked for a means of escape, but could find none. At length I saw in one of the rooms an empty wooden chest into which I jumped and pulled down the lid. But there was no escape from the barber. He came running into the room, looked right and left, and instantly guessed where I was. He was a stronger man than I thought, for he hoisted the chest onto his shoulder and carried it down the stairs. But as he rushed through the door, he tripped over the threshold, hurling me out of the chest into the crowded street. My leg was broken, but my single thought at that moment was to fly for my life. I took from my pockets handfuls of gold and threw them to the crowd. While they were busy scrambling for the coins I made off, hobbling through the back streets as fast as I could manage.

The barber pursued me, crying, 'The black-guards would have killed my master! Praise be to Allah who aided me against them and saved my master from their hands!'

Then, calling out to me as he ran, he continued, 'Now you see the fruits of your rashness and impatience! Had not Allah sent me to your rescue, you would not have escaped alive today. I have risked my life in your service; but you would not even hear of taking me with you. All the same, I will not be angry, for you are very young and exceedingly rash and foolish.'

Writhing with the pain in my leg and the anguish in my heart, I turned on my heel and threw these words at the jabbering monster: 'Is it not enough that you have brought me to this pass? Must you also hound me to my death in the middle of the market place?' Then, quickly entering a weaver's shop, I begged asylum of him and implored him to drive the barber away.

I sat in the back room prostrated with fear. I thought, 'If I return home, I will never be able to rid myself of this fiend.' I felt certain he would pursue me like a shadow, and I could endure the sight of him no longer.

I sent out for witnesses and wrote my will, dividing my property among my people. I appointed a guardian over them, and committed to him the charge of the young and the aged, and also the sale of my house and other estates. I then left Baghdad and came to live in your city, imagining that I had forever freed myself from this man. Yet no sooner had I stepped into this house than I found him sitting among you as an honored guest. How can my heart be at rest or my stay be pleasant when I am under the same roof as the man who did all this to me and was the cause of my lameness?

The young man (continued the tailor) refused to sit down and went away. When we had heard his story, we turned to the barber and asked, 'Is it true what this young man has said of you?'

'By Allah, gentlemen,' replied the barber, 'I must assure you that had it not been for my presence of mind, resourcefulness, and personal courage, this youth would have surely died. He should, indeed, be thankful that his folly cost him merely his leg, and not his life. This young man has accused me of being talkative and meddlesome – two vices from which, unlike my six brothers, I am entirely free. To prove to you the falseness of this charge, however, I will now tell you a story, and you shall judge for yourselves that I am a man not only of few words but also of great generosity and chivalry.'

THE BARBER'S TALE

The little adventure I am about to relate happened to me some years ago during the reign of our former Caliph. (May Allah have mercy upon him: he was a just ruler and a righteous man.)

One day I came across a group of ten men whom (as I discovered later) the Caliph wished to punish as rogues. He ordered his lieutenant to bring them before him. It so chanced that just as they were being taken onto a boat to cross the river Tigris I was taking the air along the river-bank. Drawing close to them, I thought to myself, 'This must be a pleasure party. They will probably spend the day in this boat eating and drinking. By Allah, I will be their guest and make merry with them.'

I jumped into the boat and sat in their midst. But as soon as we set foot on the opposite bank, the governor's guards took hold of us and put chains around the necks of the men, and around my neck also. However, I uttered not a syllable (which, I submit, is but a proof of my courage and discretion). Then they dragged us away to the Caliph's court and led us before the Commander of the Faithful.

When he saw us, the Caliph called the executioner and said to him, 'Strike off the heads of these ten wretches!'

The executioner made us kneel down in a row before the Caliph; then he unsheathed his sword and beheaded the unfortunate men.

Seeing me kneeling still at the end of the row, the Caliph cried, 'Why did you not kill the tenth man?'

The executioner counted aloud the ten heads and the ten bodies that lay on the ground – and the Caliph turned to me and said, 'Who are you, and how did you come to be among these criminals?'

Then, and only then, did I decide to break my silence.

'Commander of the Faithful,' I replied, 'I am called the Silent One and my wisdom is proverbial. I am a barber by trade and one of the seven sons of my father.' I then explained how I was mistaken for one of the prisoners and briefly outlined my life's history.

When he was satisfied that I was a man of rare qualities, the Caliph smiled, saying, 'Tell me, noble sheikh, are your six brothers like you, distinguished for their deep learning and the brevity of their speeches?'

'Gracious heavens!' I replied. 'Each of them is such a disreputable good-for-nothing that you almost slander me by comparing me to them. Because of their recklessness, stupidity, and unusual cowardice, they have brought upon themselves all kinds of misfortunes and bodily deformities: the first is lame, the second loose-limbed and disfigured, the third blind, the fourth one-eyed, and the fifth ear-cropped, and the sixth has had both his lips cut off. Were it not for the fear that you might take me for an idle gossip, I would gladly tell you their stories.'

Thereupon the Commander of the Faithful gave me leave to relate to him the story of my first brother.

THE TALE OF BAKBOOK,
THE BARBER'S FIRST BROTHER

Know, Commander of the Faithful, that the oldest
of my brothers, he who is lame, was in his youth a
tailor and lived in Baghdad.

He used to ply his trade at a little shop that he
rented from a wealthy man, who himself lived
in the upper story of the same building. In the
spacious basement below, a miller worked at his
mill and kept his ox.

One day, as he sat sewing, my brother chanced
to raise his eyes and caught sight of a young
woman looking out at the passers-by from an oriel
window above his shop. She was the landlord's

wife and was as beautiful as the rising moon. Bakbook fell in love with her at first sight. He could sew no more and passed the whole day in trying to gaze at her. Next morning he opened his shop at an early hour and began sewing; but each time he sewed a stitch, his eyes wandered toward the window and his love for the lady increased.

On the third day, she noticed him and gave him a smile. She sent her slave girl to him with a parcel containing a length of red flowered silk.

'My mistress sends you her greetings,' said the girl, 'and desires you to make her a shirt from this material.'

'I hear and obey,' replied my brother.

Bakbook set to work, so that the shirt was ready before the evening. Early next morning the slave girl came to him again and said, 'My mistress greets you and inquires if you slept well last night, for she herself, she says, could scarcely sleep a wink, thinking of you.'

Then the girl placed before him a piece of yellow satin, adding, 'From this my mistress wishes you to make her two more shirts and to have them ready by the evening.'

'I hear and obey,' replied my brother. 'Give your mistress my tender greetings, and say to her, "Your slave prostrates himself at your feet and awaits your will and pleasure."'

He worked hard until evening, when the young woman looked out from her window, smiling, so that Bakbook persuaded himself that she was deeply in love with him. Presently the slave girl came to the shop and took the two shirts.

Next morning the slave came again and said, 'My master wishes to speak to you and desires you to come into the house.'

Thinking that this was but a device to further the woman's intrigue with him, Bakbook gladly followed the slave girl, and when he entered, he greeted his landlord, kissing the ground before him. The husband threw him a great roll of silk, and said, 'Make me a few robes from this, good tailor.'

My brother went back to his shop and worked so hard that twenty robes were ready by the evening. At suppertime he carried them to his landlord.

'How much do I owe you?' asked the landlord.

But as Bakbook was about to say, 'Twenty dirhams,' the young lady made a sign to him that he should accept no payment. And the shallow-pated Bakbook, who did not for a moment suspect that the fair woman of his dreams was in league with her husband to make an ass of him, refused payment despite his poverty.

Early next morning the slave came again and said, 'My master wishes to speak with you.'

As soon as Bakbook entered, the landlord handed him a roll of stuff, saying, 'Make me five pairs of trousers.' My brother took the rascal's measurements and went back to his shop.

After three days of drudgery, he finished the

trousers; and when he proudly delivered them, the landlord complimented him on his tailoring and loaded him with praises. But just as he put his hand into his pocket to take out his purse, the young woman again signaled to Bakbook to accept no payment. So he feebly murmured a refusal and went back to his shop in exceedingly low spirits.

However, to repay Bakbook for his services, the young woman and her husband decided to marry him to their slave girl. My brother accepted without hesitation and looked forward to becoming, in a sense, a member of the family. On the evening of the wedding they advised him to spend the bridal night at the mill in the basement of the house. Nothing, they assured my brother, could be luckier than such a beginning.

After the marriage ceremony, the credulous Bakbook waited in the basement for his bride. But when she failed to come down he was obliged to sleep in that dreary place alone. At midnight he was awakened by the whip of the miller, who, at the instigation of the landlord, had tied my brother to the grinding stone during his sleep. He heard the miller's voice saying, 'A plague on this lazy ox! The corn is waiting to be ground, and the customers are demanding their flour.'

Then the miller lashed Bakbook with his whip, crying, 'Get up, and turn the mill!'

Yelling and screaming, my brother began to go around and around the millstone, and continued to do so for the rest of the night.

Early in the morning, the slave girl to whom he had been married the night before came down to the basement. Seeing him still tied to the mill-stone, she unfastened him and said with affected concern, 'We have just heard of this unfortunate mistake. My mistress cannot find words to express her grief.'

Bakbook was so overcome with exhaustion that he could not answer.

Soon after, the clerk who had drawn up the marriage contract appeared. He greeted my brother, saying, 'Allah give you a long and happy life, my friend!'

'Allah confound you!' retorted my brother. 'Your contract and blessings have only caused me to turn a mill all night.'

When the clerk heard the story of the unhappy bridegroom, he said, 'I think I know the reason. Your star is at variance with that of your bride. I can, for a small fee, draw you up a luckier contract!'

But my brother refused to listen to him and told him to go and play his tricks elsewhere.

He resumed his tailoring, hoping to make a little money with which to buy something to eat. But while he was sitting at his work, his landlord's wife appeared at the window. With tears running down her cheeks, she swore she knew nothing of what had happened at the mill that night. At first Bakbook would not believe her; but before long her sweet words won his heart again, and all his troubles were forgotten.

A few days later the slave came to him and said, 'My mistress greets you and invites you to come to her at dusk.'

Now, you must know that the young woman and her husband had conspired to ruin my brother. The landlord had said to his wife, 'How shall we entice him into the house, so that I may seize him and drag him before the governor?' And the wicked woman had answered, 'Let me play another of my tricks on him, and he shall be paraded through the city as an example to all.'

That evening my brother – a very simple-hearted man, alas – was led by the slave to the landlord's dwelling. The young woman welcomed him in and seated him by her side.

But before he could say one word to her, the husband burst into the room. He gripped my brother, crying, 'How dare you annoy my wife? By Allah, the governor himself shall judge this outrage!'

Turning a deaf ear to Bakbook's pitiful cries, he dragged him away to the governor, who had him whipped and then mounted on a camel and driven through the streets of the city. Great crowds watched the spectacle, shouting, 'Thus shall evil-doers be punished!'

During the ride Bakbook was thrown off the camel's back and broke his leg. Furthermore, the governor banished him from Baghdad. I took pity on him and carried him back in secret to my house, where I have fed and clothed him ever since.

The Caliph was much amused by my story. He ordered a gift to be bestowed upon me, saying, 'You have spoken well, my silent sheikh.'

'Commander of the Faithful,' I replied, 'I will not accept this honor until I have told you the stories of my other brothers; although, indeed, I fear that you may think me a little talkative.'

And thereupon I began to relate the tale of my second brother.

THE TALE OF AL-HADDAR,
THE BARBER'S SECOND BROTHER

My second brother, Commander of the Faithful, is called Al-Haddar and was in his younger days as thin and loose-limbed as a scarecrow.

One day, as he was slouching along the streets of Baghdad, an old woman stopped him, saying, 'I have an offer to make you, my good man. You can accept or refuse it as you think fit.'

'Tell me what it is,' said my brother.

'First,' continued the old woman, 'you must promise that you will talk but little and ask no questions.'

'Speak, then,' replied Al-Haddar.

'What would you say,' whispered the old woman, 'to a handsome house set about with beautiful gardens, where you could eat and drink to your heart's content, sitting with a pretty girl from night until day?'

'How is it, good mother,' asked Al-Haddar, 'that you have chosen me from all others to enjoy this marvel? What quality of mine has pleased you?'

'Did I not tell you,' replied the old woman, 'to ask no questions? Be silent, then, and follow me.'

My brother followed the old woman, his mouth watering at the delights she had promised him, until they came to a magnificent palace, at the doors of which stood many slaves and attendants. As he entered, my brother was stopped by one of the servants, who demanded, 'What is your business here?' But his guide promptly intervened, saying, 'He is a workman whom we have hired.'

The old woman led him up to the second story and then ushered him into a great pavilion decorated with rich ornaments. He had not waited long before a young woman of striking beauty came in, surrounded by her slave girls. Al-Haddar rose and bowed to the ground before her as she welcomed him in a most amiable fashion. When they were all seated, the slaves placed delicate sweetmeats before their mistress and her guest and, as she ate, the young woman jested with my brother and made a great show of affection to him. Although she was really laughing at him all the time, my imbecile of a brother perceived nothing and fancied that the young woman admired him greatly.

Wine was brought in, and ten beautiful girls entered the pavilion, singing to the accompaniment of lutes. The young woman plied Al-Haddar with wine, and while he drank she began to stroke his cheeks, more with violence than affection, and ended by slapping him hard on the nape of his neck. He rose angrily, and would have questioned this behavior and left the house had not the old woman reminded him, with a wink, of his promise. Determined to control himself, he sat down in silence; but no sooner had he resumed his seat than the young woman and her servants fell upon him, slapping and cuffing him until he almost fainted. Upon this Al-Haddar made up his mind that he was not to be trifled with any longer, and resolutely made for the door. But the old woman hastened to prevent him.

'How long,' he asked, 'have I to sit here? Never in all the days of my life have I been so vilely treated.'

Nevertheless the old woman prevailed upon him to stay in the pavilion.

Presently the young woman ordered her slaves to perfume my brother and sprinkle his face with rose water. When they had done so, she called one of her slave girls and said, 'Take your master and do to him what is required. Then bring him back.'

Not knowing what lay in store for him, my brother allowed himself to be conducted into a neighboring room. The old woman soon joined him and said, 'Be patient.'

'Tell me,' said Al-Haddar, his face brightening, 'what does she want the slave to do to me?'

'Nothing but good,' replied the old woman. 'She will only dye your eyebrows and shave off your mustache.'

'As for the dyeing of my eyebrows,' said Al-Haddar, 'that will come off with washing; it is the shaving of my mustache that I cannot endure.'

'Beware of crossing her,' replied the old woman.

My brother patiently suffered the slave girl to dye his eyebrows and remove his mustache. But when the girl returned to her mistress to inform her that her instructions had been carried out, the young woman said, 'There remains only one other thing to be done: his beard must be shaved off.' So the slave went back to him and told him of his hostess' orders.

'How can I allow this to happen to me?' said the blockhead, deeply perplexed.

But the old woman answered, 'Be a little more patient, and you will win her.'

So my brother hopefully let the slave girl shave off his beard. When he was brought back, the company was so amused by his grotesque appearance that they rolled on the floor with laughter.

The young woman whispered in his ear, 'Run

after me until you catch me!' With this she tripped out of the pavilion and rushed in and out of many rooms and galleries, Al-Haddar following close behind. At length she slipped into a darkened chamber, and as he was scampering after her the floor suddenly gave way beneath him. In a twinkling he found himself below in the market of the leather merchants.

On seeing Al-Haddar drop down in their midst, his beard shaven and his eyebrows dyed, the merchants booed him, clapped their hands at him, and thrashed him with their hides, until he collapsed senseless. Finally they threw him on a donkey's back and took him to the governor, who asked, 'Who can this man be?'

'He fell down upon us,' they answered, 'through a trap door in the vizier's house.'

The governor sentenced him to a hundred lashes and banished him from the city. As soon as this news reached me, I set out to search for him, and when I found him brought him back in secret to Baghdad and made him a daily allowance of food and drink. Were it not for my generosity and courage, I would not have gone to so much trouble over such a fool.

I now beg you, Commander of the Faithful, to listen to the story of my third brother.

THE TALE OF BAKBAK,
THE BARBER'S THIRD BROTHER

My third brother, Commander of the Faithful, is
the blind one called Bakbak.

One day, as he was begging in the streets of
Baghdad, destiny directed his steps to a certain
house. He knocked at the door, hoping that he
might be given a coin or something to eat. The
master of the house called out from within, 'Who
is there?' But my brother, who knew all the tricks
of his profession, would not answer before the
door was opened. Again he heard the master of
the house call out at the top of his voice, 'Who is
knocking?' and still he made no reply. Bakbak

then heard the sound of approaching footsteps, and the door was opened.

'What do you want?' he was asked.

'Some little thing for a poor blind man, in the name of Allah,' replied my brother.

'Give me your hand,' said the man, 'and follow me.'

Bakbak stretched out his hand, and was taken within and then up from one flight of stairs to another until the roof of the house was reached, my brother thinking at every step that he was about to be given some food or money. On the roof the man asked Bakbak a second time, 'Now, what do you want?'

'Some little thing,' repeated my brother, 'in the name of Allah.'

'Then may Allah have pity on you,' replied the man, 'and open a door for you elsewhere.'

'Could you not have given me that answer when we were still below?' cried my brother indignantly.

'Wretch,' retorted the master of the house, 'why did you not tell me who you were when I first asked you?'

'What are you doing with me?' asked my brother helplessly.

'I have nothing to give you,' the man answered.

'Then guide me down the stairs,' pleaded Bakbak.

'The way lies open before you,' answered the man coldly.

Unaided, my brother groped his way down the stairs. But when he was some twenty steps from the bottom his foot slipped, and he rolled down nearly all the way, breaking his skull.

Outside the house, two of his fellow blind beggars heard his groans and went to ask him what had happened. Dolefully he described the treatment he had received, adding, 'Comrades, there is no way left for me but to go to our house and take something from our common savings; or else I shall be hungry for the rest of this black day.'

Now all this time, the man from whose house my brother had been so rudely thrown out was following Bakbak and his blind companions and overheard all that they said to each other. He continued walking quietly behind them until they reached their dwelling. When the three had entered, he slipped into the house without a sound.

'Shut the door quickly,' said my brother to his friends, 'and search the house lest any strangers should have followed us.'

When he heard my brother's words, the man, who was an accomplished thief, noiselessly caught a rope that was hanging from the ceiling, and, climbing it, held fast until the blind men had inspected every corner. They then brought out their money and, sitting down beside my brother, began counting it; and there were more than twelve thousand coins. This done, one of them took a coin and hurried out of the house to buy something to eat, while the other two put back the silver in its hiding place under the tiles. As soon as their companion returned, all three sat down to eat.

During the meal my brother gradually became aware of a fourth pair of jaws chewing by his side. 'There is a stranger in our midst!' shouted Bakbak. He stretched out his hand and groped around him. It fell on the thief.

The three blind men closed upon the stranger, punching and kicking him, and crying out, 'A thief! Help, good Moslems! A thief, help!'

When the neighbors and passers-by came to their rescue, the thief shut his eyes, pretending to be blind like the three beggars. 'Take me to the governor, good Moslems,' he cried out 'for, by Allah, I have important information to give him.'

At once the crowd seized the four and led them to the governor's house.

'Who are these men?' asked the governor.

'Noble Governor,' cried the thief, 'nothing but the whip can make us confess the truth. Begin by flogging me, and then these others!'

'Throw this man down and thrash him soundly,' said the governor.

The guards seized the pretender and set upon him with their whips. After the first few lashes, he yelled and opened one of his eyes; and after a few more he opened the other.

'Wicked impostor,' cried the governor, 'so you are not blind after all!'

'Grant me your pardon,' begged the thief, 'and I will tell you the whole truth.'

The Governor nodded assent, and the man continued, 'For a long time we four have pretended to be blind beggars, entering the houses of honest men and cheating them of their money. We amassed a large fortune, amounting to twelve thousand dirhams in silver. But when I demanded my share today they rose against me and beat me. I beg protection of Allah and of you; and if, noble Governor, you doubt the truth of my confession, put them to the whip and they will open their eyes.'

'Scoundrels!' roared the governor. 'Dare you deny Allah's most precious gift and pretend to be blind?'

The first to suffer was my brother. In vain he swore, by Allah and by all that is holy, that only one of them was blessed with sight. They continued to whip him until he fainted.

'Leave him until he comes to,' cried the governor, 'and then whip him again!'

The others received similar treatment; nor did they open their eyes in spite of the impostor's repeated exhortations. Then the governor sent his guards to fetch the money from my brother's house. A quarter of it he gave to the thief, and kept the remainder for himself. Furthermore, he banished Bakbak and his friends from the city.

When I heard of my brother's misfortunes I set

out to search for him and brought him back in
secret to my house, where he has lived ever since.

The Caliph laughed heartily at my story, and
said to his attendants, 'Give him a reward and
show him out of the palace.'

'By Allah,' I replied, 'I will accept nothing,
Commander of the Faithful, until you have heard
the stories of my other brothers.'

THE TALE OF AL-KUZ,
THE BARBER'S FOURTH BROTHER

My fourth brother, one-eyed Al-Kuz, was at one time a butcher and sheep breeder in Baghdad. He catered to the rich and the highborn, so that he amassed great wealth and in time became an owner of many herds of cattle and large estates.

He continued to prosper until a certain day when, as he was attending to his customers, an old man with a long white beard entered the shop and asked him to weigh him some mutton. My brother did so, and when he examined the coins that he received from the stranger he was so struck by their unusual brilliance that he kept them in a separate coffer. For five months the old man bought meat regularly from my brother, who, each time he was paid, put the bright new coins aside.

One day, wishing to buy some sheep, my brother opened the coffer and found, to his astonishment and dismay, that it was filled only with little pellets of white paper. He set up a great clamor, beating himself about the head and calling out to passers-by, until a huge crowd gathered around him. While he was telling them his story, the old man himself came forward with the glittering coins ready in his hand, as was his custom. My brother sprang upon him and, taking him by the throat, cried, 'Help, good people! Here is the scoundrel who has robbed me!'

But this did not seem to perturb the old man, who calmly whispered to my brother, 'Hold your tongue, or I will put you to public shame!'

'And how will you do that?' shouted Al-Kuz.

'By charging you here and now with selling human flesh for mutton!'

'You lie, accursed swindler!' yelled my brother.

'None is more accursed,' rejoined the other, 'than the man who at this moment has a human corpse hung up in his shop instead of a sheep!'

'If you can prove this crime against me,' said Al-Kuz, 'my life and all my property are yours!'

Accepting the challenge, the old man turned to the bystanders and cried, 'Good Moslems, for months this butcher has been slaughtering his fellow men and selling us their flesh as mutton. If anyone doubts this, let him enter the shop and see for himself!'

The crowd rushed in, and what should they see hanging from one of the hooks but the corpse of a man! Struck with horror, the infuriated mob attacked Al-Kuz, crying, 'Criminal! Murderer!' Even those who were his oldest clients and dearest friends turned against him and beat him. In the hubbub, the sorcerer (for such was the wicked old man) struck my brother in the face, knocking out his left eye.

Then the crowd carried him and the supposed corpse to the chief of the city's magistrates.

'Your honor,' said the sorcerer, 'we bring before you a criminal who for months has been murdering human beings and selling their flesh as mutton. We call upon you to administer Allah's justice; and here are all the witnesses.'

My brother tried to defend himself, but the judge would not listen to him and sentenced him to five hundred lashes. He confiscated all his goods and banished him from the city. Indeed, had Al-Kuz been a poor man he would have been put to a cruel death.

Penniless and broken, he left Baghdad and journeyed many days and nights until he arrived in the chief city of a foreign land. There he set up as a cobbler, making a precarious living in a small shop.

While walking along the street one day he heard

the neighing of many horses and a loud clatter of hoofs and was curious to know what was happening. Upon inquiry he was informed that the King was going hunting, so he stopped to watch the procession pass. Chancing to glance over his shoulder, the King caught sight of my brother's face and with a start turned away his head, crying, 'Allah preserve us from the evil eye and from the portent of this day!' At once he turned his horse about and rode back to his palace, followed by the troops. As for my brother, he was set upon by the King's slaves and beaten, and then left for dead by the roadside.

Al-Kuz was so perplexed at this stroke of ill-fortune that he took himself off to one of the King's attendants and told him what had happened. The courtier burst into a fit of laughter, and said, 'The King cannot bear the sight of a one-eyed man, especially if it is the left eye that is missing. Indeed, in this land, death is the usual penalty for such a disfigurement.'

When Al-Kuz heard this he decided to flee the country, and set out at once for a far-off town where no one knew him. Many months afterward, as he was taking a walk, he suddenly heard in the distance the neighing of horses and the clatter of hoofs. He took to his heels in great panic, searching in vain for a hiding place. At length he found himself on the threshold of a great door and, pushing it open without a moment's thought, entered a long passage. Scarcely had he advanced one step when two men sprang upon him, crying, 'Allah be praised that we have caught you at last! We have passed three sleepless nights in fear of you!'

'But, good people,' cried my brother, 'what have I done to offend you?'

'You are the one-eyed ruffian who has plotted to kill the master of this house and to ruin us all!' they cried. 'Was it not enough that you robbed him of his property, you and your friends? Where is the dagger with which you threatened us yesterday?' So saying, they searched Al-Kuz and found his cobbler's knife in his belt.

'Good people,' pleaded my brother, 'Fear Allah and let me tell you my story!'

But instead of listening to him, they beat him and tore his clothes to tatters. His body being uncovered, the marks of whipping could be seen on his back. 'Dog!' they cried. 'These scars bear testimony to your other crimes!' Then they dragged him away to the governor.

My brother tried to speak out in his own defense, but the governor turned a deaf ear to his entreaties. 'Wretch!' he cried indignantly. 'One need only look upon your back to see that you have practiced every kind of crime!' and he ordered that he be given a hundred lashes.

Then the governor's men hoisted Al-Kuz on the back of a camel and drove him through the streets, crying, 'Thus shall house-breaking ruffians be punished.'

When I heard of my brother's misfortunes, I searched for him until I found him and then brought him back in secret to Baghdad, where he has lived under my care and protection ever since.

That is the story of Al-Kuz. But do not think, Commander of the Faithful, that it is in any way more extraordinary than the tale of my fifth brother.

THE TALE OF AL-ASHAR,
THE BARBER'S FIFTH BROTHER

My fifth brother is called Al-Ashar In his youth
he was very poor and used to beg alms by night
and spend the proceeds by day. When our father
died, we each inherited a hundred pieces of silver.
For many weeks Al-Ashar did not know what to
do with his share, and at length he decided to be a
glass merchant. He bought some glassware with
his hundred dirhams and, placing the articles in a
large basket, sat with it at a corner in a busy
thoroughfare.

On a certain Friday, while squatting in his
accustomed place, he sank into a reverie, and

thought to himself, 'I have invested the whole of my capital in this glassware. It cost me a hundred dirhams and I will no doubt sell it for two hundred. With the two hundred I will buy more glass, which I will sell for four hundred. I will go on buying and selling until I make a large fortune. With this I will buy all kinds of essences and jewelry, and make a vast profit. Then I will be able to afford a splendid house, with slaves, and horses, and gilded saddles. I will eat the choicest dishes, drink the rarest wines, and be entertained in my own house by the sweetest singers of the city.

'When I have made a hundred thousand dirhams, I will send for the most knowledgeable marriage brokers and instruct them to find me a wife among the daughters of kings and viziers. I will perhaps ask for the hand of the Grand Vizier's daughter, for I hear she is a girl of incomparable beauty. I will offer a marriage portion of a thousand pieces of gold; and should her father withhold his consent, I will carry her away by force. I will buy ten young eunuchs to attend upon me, and dress myself in regal robes. My saddle will be adorned with priceless jewels, and as I ride through the city to the Vizier's house with slaves before me and servants behind me, men will bow reverently as I pass by, greeting and blessing me.

'When I enter the vizier's house, he will stand up to receive me. He will give me his own place and sit himself down at my feet. Two of my slaves

will carry purses with a thousand dinars in each;
one I will lay before the vizier as his daughter's
marriage portion, the other I will present to him
as a gift, in proof of my worthiness and munifi-
cence. I will be solemn and reserved, and for
every ten words he addresses to me I will answer
with two. Then I will return to my house. And
when one of my future wife's relations returns my
visit, I will give him gold and a robe of honor; but
if he brings me a present, I will return it to him,
so that he will know how proud my spirit is.

'I will myself appoint the wedding day, and
then make preparations for the bridal festivities.
On the wedding night I will put on my most
splendid robes and, surrounded by my guests,
will recline upon a mattress of gold brocade. I will
turn my head neither to the right nor to the left,
but will look straight in front of me with an air of
authority and contemptuous unconcern. When my
bride is brought before me, decked with jewels
and radiant like the full moon, I will not even look
at her. Her women will plead with me, saying,
"Our lord and master, here stands your wife, your
slave, waiting for you to honor her with a gracious
look." They will kiss the ground before me. I will
cast one glance at her and resume my disdainful
air. They will then conduct her to the bridal
chamber. I will order one of my slaves to bring
me five hundred pieces of gold, which I will
scatter among my wife's attendants. Then I will
go to my bride; and when I am left alone with her

I will neither speak to her nor even look at her. Presently the bride's mother will come in, kissing my head and hand, and saying, "My lord, look upon your slave girl, who yearns for your favor; speak to her and heal her broken spirit." I will make no answer. She will throw herself down at my feet, saying, "Your slave is a beautiful girl. On my knees I beg you to cease humbling her, or her heart will break!" Then the bride's mother will rise and, filling a cup with wine, will give it to her daughter, who will offer it to me with all submission. But I, leaning idly upon my elbow among the gold-embroidered cushions, will take no notice of her. With a trembling voice she will say, "I beg you, my lord, to take this cup from the hand of your slave and servant." But I will maintain my dignified silence. She will raise the cup to my mouth, pressing me to drink from it. Then I will wave it away with my hand, and spurn her with my foot, thus –'

So saying, Al-Ashar moved his foot, which kicked against the basket of glassware, knocking over the contents and sending them crashing in fragments to the ground.

My brother began to beat himself about the face, tearing his clothes and wailing, as the people went by to the midday prayers. Some stopped to say a kind word to him and some passed by, taking no notice of his lamentation. While he sat bitterly mourning the loss of all his worldly possessions, a woman rode by on her way to the mosque.

She was very beautiful, and as she passed, surrounded by her servants, a sweet odor of the rarest musk hung about her. Moved with pity for my brother, she sent to inquire the cause of his distress. When she heard his story, she called one of her servants and said, 'Give this unfortunate man the purse you are carrying.'

The servant took from his belt a heavy purse and gave it to Al-Ashar, who, on opening it, found that it contained five hundred pieces of gold. He almost died for joy and fervently called down Allah's blessing on his benefactress.

Carrying the great purse, my brother returned to his house a rich man. He sat thinking of the happy turn of his fortune, and was on the point of conjuring up another vision when he was roused by a knocking at the door. He opened it and found an old woman on the threshold whom he had never seen before.

'My son,' said the old woman, 'the hour of Friday prayers is almost past, and I have not yet washed my hands and feet as custom requires. I beg you to let me come into your house, so that I may prepare myself.'

Al-Ashar politely invited her to enter. He brought her a ewer and a basin, and retired to delight his eyes with his treasure.

A few minutes afterward the old woman appeared in the room where my brother was sitting. She knelt and bowed twice in prayer, and called down blessings on my brother. He thanked her, took two dinars from the purse, and offered them to her. But the old woman refused the gold with dignity, saying, 'Put this money back into your purse. If you have no need of it, return it to the lady who gave it to you.'

'Do you know her?' asked Al-Ashar in a transport of joy. 'I beg you to tell me how I can see her again.'

'My son,' she replied, 'I have served that lady for many years. I assure you that she has a great liking for you. Rise, take with you all your money lest a thief should steal it, and follow me to the lady's house.'

Bursting with happiness, Al-Ashar rose, took all his gold, and followed the old woman until she stopped at a great house and knocked. The door was opened by a Greek slave girl, and the old woman went in, followed by my brother. Al-Ashar soon found himself in a spacious hall, hung with rich tapestry and spread with rare carpets. He sat down on a cushion, holding his turban on his knees, and had not waited long before a young woman, attired in splendid silks and blessed with more loveliness than the eyes of men had ever seen, appeared before him.

Al-Ashar rose to his feet as she entered, and when she saw him she welcomed him with a sweet smile. They sat talking for a few moments. Then the young woman rose, saying, 'Stay here until I return.'

While my brother was waiting, the door was

flung wide open and there entered a tall slave, holding an unsheathed sword in his hand.

'Vilest of men,' cried the slave, 'who brought you to this house, and what are you doing here?'

My brother's tongue stuck in his throat and he did not know what to answer. The slave took hold of him and beat him with the flat of his sword until he fell down unconscious. Taking him for dead, the slave called out for the old woman, who instantly appeared.

She took his purse of gold, then gripped Al-Ashar by the feet, dragged him out of the room, and pushed him into a dark cellar.

For two days he remained there unconscious. After he came to, and his strength had returned a little, Al-Ashar crawled on all fours groping for the door. Having at length found it, he made his way, with Allah's help, from the cellar to the vestibule, where he concealed himself. Next morning the old woman went out in search of another victim; and before she had time to shut the door behind her, my brother slipped out and ran home as fast as his legs could carry him.

He now began to plan a punishment for the old woman and her accomplices. Keeping a watchful eye on her movements, he acquainted himself with her daily haunts. As soon as he was restored to his normal health he disguised himself as a traveler from a foreign land. To his waist he tied a large bag filled with glass fragments as though it were bursting with coins, and hiding a sword under his robe went out to seek the old woman.

On finding her, Al-Ashar addressed her in an uncouth foreign accent, 'Good mother, have you a pair of scales in which I can weigh nine hundred pieces of gold? I am a stranger here and do not know anyone in this city.'

The old woman answered, 'One of my sons is a money-changer and has all kinds of scales. He will gladly weigh your gold for you.'

My brother followed her until she stopped at the door of the sinister house. The young woman herself opened it for them, and the old servant whispered, 'I have brought you a good catch today.' The young woman led my brother in, as before, and presently the slave appeared with his naked sword.

'Get up,' he roared, 'and follow me!'

My brother rose, and as the slave turned his back, Al-Ashar drew his sword, sprang upon him, and struck off his head with one blow.

He next called out to the old woman, and when she appeared he cried, 'Black-souled hag, do you not recognize me?'

'I do not indeed,' she replied.

'Know, then,' shouted my brother, 'that I am the man to whose house you came to wash your hands and feet, and whom you betrayed so wickedly!'

The old woman implored him on her knees to pardon her, but with one stroke of his sword Al-

Ashar cut her in two pieces. He then set out to look for her mistress. When he found her, the terrified young woman entreated him to spare her life. His heart was softened, and he pardoned her.

'How did you fall into the power of that cruel slave?' he asked.

'Three years ago,' she replied, 'before I was imprisoned in this house, I was a slave in the service of a merchant of this city. A frequent visitor at our house was the old woman. One day she invited me to accompany her to an entertainment. I accepted gladly, and, putting on my best clothes and taking with me a purse of one hundred dinars, went out with her. She led me to this house, where that man has kept me and made me the instrument of his crimes ever since.'

Al-Ashar ordered her to conduct him to the place where the stolen gold was hidden. He stood dumbfounded as she opened coffer after coffer, all filled with glittering coins.

'You will never be able to carry all this gold alone,' she said. 'Go and bring some porters to take it from the house.'

Al-Ashar left at once and soon returned with ten strong men. But he found the doors wide open and the girl and most of the money gone. He realized that the young woman had deceived him. Nevertheless, he contented himself with what she had left behind. He emptied the closets of their valuables and took everything home.

Al-Ashar slept in great happiness that night.

But when he woke next morning, he was terrified to find twenty of the governor's guards at his door. They seized him, saying, 'You are wanted by our master.'

The men dragged him before the governor, who asked, 'Whence did you steal all this money and these goods?'

'Noble Governor,' replied Al-Ashar, 'grant me the pledge of mercy, and I will tell you the whole truth.'

The Governor threw him the white handkerchief signifying pardon. My brother related to him the story of his adventures and offered him a handsome share of the spoil. But the governor seized everything for himself and, fearing that the Caliph might hear of his action, decided to get rid of my brother by banishing him from the city.

Thus Al-Ashar was forced to leave Baghdad. But he had not traveled far before he was set upon by a band of highwaymen, who, finding that they could not rob him of anything except his rags, beat him mercilessly and cut off both his ears.

When I heard of my brother's misfortunes, Commander of the Faithful, I set out to search for him and, having found him, brought him back in secret to my house, where I have provided for him ever since.

That is the story of Al-Ashar. I will now tell you

the tale of my sixth and last brother, which, as you will readily agree, is even more extraordinary than the other tales.

The Tale of Shakashik,
the Barber's Sixth Brother

My sixth brother, Commander of the Faithful, is called Shakashik. In his youth he was very poor. One day, when he was begging in the streets of Baghdad, he noticed a splendid mansion, at the gates of which stood an impressive band of attendants. Upon inquiry he was informed that the house belonged to a member of the wealthy and powerful Barmecide family. Shakashik approached the doorkeeper and begged for alms.

'Go in,' they said, 'and our master will give you all that you desire.'

My brother entered the lofty vestibule and proceeded to a spacious marble-paved hall, hung with tapestry and overlooking a beautiful garden. He stood bewildered for a moment, not knowing where to turn his steps, and then advanced to the far end of the hall. There, among the cushions, reclined a handsome old man with a long beard, who, my brother saw at a glance, was the master of the house.

'What can I do for you, my friend?' asked the old man, as he rose to welcome my brother.

When Shakashik explained that he was a hungry beggar, the old man expressed the deepest compassion and rent his fine robes, crying, 'Can there be a man as hungry as yourself in a city where I am living? It is, indeed a disgrace that I cannot endure!' Then he comforted my brother, adding, 'I insist that you stay here and partake of dinner with me.'

With this the master of the house clapped his hands and called out to one of the slaves, 'Bring in the basin and ewer.' Then he said to my brother, 'Come forward, my friend, and wash your hands.'

Shakashik rose to wash his hands, but saw neither ewer nor basin. He was bewildered to see his host make gestures as though he were pouring water on his hands from an invisible vessel and then drying them with an invisible towel. When he had finished, the old man called out to his attendants, 'Bring in the table!'

Numerous servants hurried in and out of the hall, as though they were preparing for a meal.

My brother could still see nothing. Yet his host invited him to sit at the imaginary table, saying, 'Honor me by eating of this meat.'

He moved his hands about as though he were touching invisible dishes, and also moved his jaws and lips as though he were chewing. Then said he to Shakashik, 'Eat your fill, my friend, for you must be famished.'

My brother began to move his jaws, to chew and swallow, as though he were eating, while the old man still coaxed him, saying, 'Eat, my friend, and note the excellence of this bread and its whiteness.'

'This man,' thought Shakashik, 'must be fond of practical jokes.' So he said, 'It is, sir, the whitest bread I have ever seen, and I have never tasted the like of it in all my life.'

'This bread,' said the host, 'was baked by a slave girl whom I bought for five hundred dinars.' Then he called out to one of his slaves, 'Bring in the meat pudding, and let there be plenty of fat in it!'

Turning to my brother, he continued, 'By Allah, my friend, have you ever tasted anything better than this meat pudding? Now, on my life, you must eat and be merry!'

Presently he cried out again, 'Serve up the stewed grouse!' And again he said to Shakashik, 'Eat your fill, my friend, for you must be very hungry.'

My brother moved his jaws, and chewed, and

swallowed, while the old man went on calling
for one imaginary dish after another, and pressing his guest to partake of them. He ordered,
'Serve up the chickens stuffed with pistachio
nuts,' and turned to Shakashik, saying, 'Eat, for
you have never tasted anything like these
chickens!'

'Sir,' replied my brother, 'they are indeed incom-
parably delicious.' Thereupon the host moved his
fingers as though to pick up a morsel from an
imaginary dish, and popped the invisible delicacy
into my brother's mouth.

He continued to enlarge upon the excellence of
the various dishes, while my brother became so
ravenously hungry that he would almost have
given his life for a crust of barley bread.

'Have you ever tasted anything more delicious?'
asked the old man, 'than the spices in these
dishes?'

'Never,' replied Shakashik.

'Eat heartily, then, and do not be ashamed!'

'I thank you, sir,' answered Shakashik, 'but I
have already eaten my fill.'

'Bring in the dessert!' cried the master of the
house to a servant; and to my brother he said,
'Taste this excellent pastry, eat of these fritters –
take this one before the syrup drips out of it!'

Shakashik helped himself to the imperceptible
dainty, and, clicking his tongue with delight, re-
marked upon the abundance of spice in it.

'Yes,' agreed the old man, 'I always insist on a

dinar's weight of spice in each fritter, and half that quantity of honey.'

My brother continued to move his jaws and lips and to roll his tongue between his cheeks, as though he were enjoying the sumptuous feast.

'Eat of these roasted almonds, and walnuts, and raisins,' said the old man.

'I can eat no more,' replied my brother.

'By Allah!' repeated the host. 'You must eat and not remain hungry!'

'Sir,' protested Shakashik, 'how can one remain hungry after eating all these dishes?'

My poor brother considered the manner in which his host was making game of him, and thought, 'By Allah, I will do something that will make him repent of his pranks!'

Presently, however, the old man clapped his hands again and cried, 'Bring in the wine!'

Numerous slaves ran in, moving their hands about as though they were setting wine and cups before their master and his guest. The old man pretended to pour wine into the cups and to hand one to my brother. 'Take this,' he said, 'and tell me how you like '

'Sir,' replied Shakashik, lifting the invisible cup to his lips and making as if to drain it at one gulp, 'your generosity overwhelms me!'

'Health and joy to you!' exclaimed the host, as he pretended to pour himself some wine and drink it off. He handed another cup to his guest, and they both continued to act in this fashion until

Shakashik, feigning himself drunk, began to roll his head from side to side. Then, taking his host unawares, he suddenly raised his arm and dealt him a blow on the neck that made the hall echo with the sound. And this he followed by a second blow.

The old man rose in anger and cried, 'What are you doing, vile creature?'

'Sir,' replied my brother, 'you have received your humble slave into your home and loaded him with your generosity. You have fed him with the choicest food and quenched his thirst with the most potent wines. Alas, he became drunk, and forgot his manners! But you are so noble, sir, that you will surely pardon his offense.'

At these words, the old man burst out laughing, and said, 'For a long time I have jested with all types of men, but no one has ever had the patience or wit to enter into my humors as you have done. Now, therefore, I pardon you, and ask you in truth to eat and drink with me, and to be my companion for as long as I live.'

He ordered his attendants to serve all the dishes that they had consumed in fancy, and when he and my brother had eaten their fill they repaired to the drinking chamber, where beautiful young women sang and made music. The old Barmecide gave Shakashik a robe of honor and made him his constant companion.

The two lived in amity for a period of twenty years, until the old man died and the Caliph seized all his property. My brother was forced to fly for his life. He left Baghdad and rode into the desert. There a band of roving bedouin took him prisoner and carried him away to their encampment. Every day their chieftain put him to the torture and threatened him, saying, 'Pay us your ransom or I will kill you!' My brother would weep and swear that he was a penniless outcast. Finally the chieftain cut off both his lips, then took him on a camel to a barren hillside and left him there to perish.

However, Shakashik was rescued by some travelers who recognized him and gave him food and drink. When news of his plight reached me, I journeyed to him and brought him back to Baghdad. I nursed him in my own house and have provided for him ever since.

When he had heard the tale of my sixth brother (continued the barber, finishing the story he was relating at the tradesmen's party), the Caliph Al-Muntasir Billah burst out laughing and said, 'I can well see, my silent friend, that you are a man of few words, who knows neither curiosity nor indiscretion. Yet I must ask you to leave this city at once and go to live elsewhere.'

Thus, for no conceivable reason, the Caliph banished me from Baghdad.

I journeyed through many foreign lands until I heard of Al-Muntasir's death and the succession of another Caliph. Then I returned to Baghdad, and found that all my brothers had died also. It was soon after my return that I met this young man, whom I saved from certain death, and who has so unjustly accused me of being talkative and officious.

Your Majesty (continued the tailor), after hearing the barber we were all convinced that the lame young man had been the victim of an exceptionally garrulous and meddlesome fellow. We therefore decided to punish him; so we seized him and locked him in an empty room. Then we sat in peace, eating and drinking and making merry until the hour of afternoon prayers.

When I returned home, my wife received me with angry looks.

'A fine husband you are,' she burst out, 'to enjoy yourself all day while your wife sits moping all alone at home. If you do not take me out at once and entertain me, I will divorce you!'

We went out together and passed the rest of the day in search of amusement. As we were returning home in the evening we met the hunchback whose untimely death has caused all this company to assemble here.

The King of Basra was much amused by the tailor's story and said, 'The young man's adventure with the barber certainly surpasses in wonder the story of the hunchback.' And, turning to the chamberlain and the tailor, he added, 'Go seek the barber and bring him before me. We will then bury the hunchback, for he has been dead since yesterday.'

The two men hurried to the house where the barber was still imprisoned. They set him free and brought him before the King, who discovered that he was an old man past his seventieth year, with dark complexion, a long white beard, and gray, bushy eyebrows; his nose was long, his ears were shriveled, and his manner was lofty. Having looked him over well, the King burst into a fit of laughter, saying, 'Silent One, we wish to hear some of your stories.'

'First, your Majesty,' replied the barber, 'I would myself wish to know the occasion for this gathering and why the hunchback's body lies before you.'

The King said to the company, 'Tell the barber the story of the hunchback's death, and all that befell him at the hands of the tailor, the doctor, the steward, and the broker.'

When he had heard all, the barber exclaimed, 'By Allah, this is very strange! Lift the cover from the hunchback's body, and let me examine it.'

They removed the cover, and the barber, having sat down, took the hunchback's head upon his knees. After scrutinizing the face for a while, he burst out laughing and exclaiming, 'Death is one of Allah's mysteries; but the death of this hunchback is a wonder that ought to be recorded for all time!'

The King and all the company were astonished by his words.

'Explain your meaning,' said the King.

'Your Majesty,' came the reply, 'the hunchback is alive!'

So saying, the barber took from his belt a vial containing an ointment, with which he rubbed the hunchback's neck. Then, producing a pair of iron forceps from his pocket, he inserted it into the hunchback's throat and pulled out the piece of fish with the bone. With a violent sneeze the hunchback sprang to his feet. He passed his hands over his face and said, 'There is no god but Allah, and Mohammed is his prophet.'

The King and all the company marveled greatly. 'By Allah,' exclaimed the King, 'I have never in all my life heard of a stranger incident than this!' Then, turning to the captains of his army, he added, 'Have any of you, good Moslems, ever seen a dead man come to life in this fashion? Had not Allah sent him this barber, our hunchback would have now been counted among the dead.'

And all those present said, 'By Allah, it is a rare marvel!'

The King ordered that the incident be recorded on parchment and that the scroll be kept in the royal library. He bestowed robe's of honor upon the Jew, the Christian, the steward, the tailor, the hunchback, and the barber. He appointed the tailor to his court, endowed him with a large annuity, and reconciled him with the hunchback, who again became the King's drinking companion. The barber he also appointed to his court, and conferred upon him many honors, and made him a favorite companion. And they all lived happily until they were visited by the Destroyer of all earthly pleasures, the Annihilator of men.

ALI BABA AND THE FORTY THIEVES

Long ago there lived in a city of Persia two brothers whose names were Kassim and Ali Baba.

Though born of the same parents and brought up in the same home, their characters were quite different. Kassim, the elder, was arrogant, shrewd, and greedy, while Ali Baba was unassuming, kind-hearted, and content with his situation. When their father died, they divided all he had between them and started life on an equal footing, but while Kassim married a rich wife and became the owner of a thriving shop in the city's main bazaar, Ali Baba took to wife the daughter humble family, and earned a modest living by cutting wood in the forest and selling it in the town.

Ali Baba lived frugally and wisely with his wife, saving as much as his earnings would allow, so that in a few months he was able to buy three donkeys. Every day he would lead his donkeys to the forest and bring them back laden with firewood.

One day, while working at the edge of a far thicket, with his donkeys grazing peacefully near by, he heard the clatter of galloping hoofs in the distance and saw a great cloud of dust approaching. Curious to find out the cause of the commotion, he climbed cautiously into a tall tree that stood on a hillside, giving a clear view of the adjacent plain. From his hiding place he saw a troop of fierce-looking armed horsemen riding toward him. He counted forty of them, and guessed from their appearance and demeanor – their fiery eyes, their black, pointed beards, and the weapons they carried – that they were a band of robbers.

When they came under the tree, the forty thieves dismounted at a signal from the captain and started removing their saddlebags. They carried their loads to a great rock at the bottom of the hill; then the captain went up to the rock and in a loud voice cried, 'Open, Sesame!'

Ali Baba was astonished to notice that, at the mention of this word – the name of a cereal commonly grown in Persia – a hidden door in the rock swung wide open. The entire band of robbers filed in. In a few moments they emerged, carrying their now-empty saddlebags in their hands, and the captain cried, 'Close, Sesame!' The rock at once shut behind them, and no one could have guessed there was any opening in that solid surface.

As soon as the robbers had mounted and ridden off, Ali Baba climbed down from the tree and went up to the mysterious rock. Finding the surface as smooth and solid as before, he marveled at the magic that had forced it open.

'What priceless treasures must lie within it!' he reflected, and, remembering the captain's words, decided to utter them himself and see what would happen.

'Open, Sesame!' he shouted.

The rock opened, just as it had done before, and Ali Baba walked in. Being a good Moslem, he murmured as he entered, 'In the name of Allah, the Compassionate, the Merciful!' He found himself in a huge cave piled up with rich ornaments, chests brimful with gold and silver coins, and great bags bursting with precious stones – which must have taken hundreds of years to accumulate. As he scanned the vast treasures, Ali Baba realized that the cave was the secret storehouse of countless generations of thieves and highwaymen.

Carefully choosing six bags of gold, he loaded them on his donkeys and covered them with brushwood to hide them. Then he cried aloud, 'Close, Sesame!' and in a twinkling the door slid to behind him, leaving not a trace on the rock's outer surface.

When Ali Baba arrived home and his wife saw him unload the bags of gold, she was seized with shame and fear.

'Good husband,' she said, 'do not tell me you have earned all this gold by cutting wood in the forest. Bad luck is sure to enter our humble house if we keep such ill-gotten gains here.'

'Fear nothing, I am no thief,' Ali Baba quickly interrupted. 'Rather rejoice, for it was Allah who guided my footsteps in the forest this morning.' And he told her of his adventure and how he had found the gold in the robbers' hide-out.

When she heard the story, the poor woman was filled with relief and joy. She squatted before the pile of gold that her husband had poured out of the bags and tried to value the incalculable coins.

'Don't try to count them,' said Ali Baba with a laugh. 'It would take you days to do that. Get up now and help me dig a ditch in the kitchen where we can hide them. To leave them here would only rouse the suspicions of our neighbors.'

But his wife wanted to know exactly how rich they were. 'If I cannot count them,' she said, 'I must at least weigh or measure them. I will go and borrow a measure from your brother Kassim's house, and then I can measure the gold while you dig the hole.'

She went over to Kassim's house across the lane and begged his wife to lend her a measure.

'You can have one,' her sister-in-law replied. But she wondered at the same time why Ali Baba should need a measure when he was so poor that he could buy only a day's supply of wheat at a time. So the cunning woman, curious to know what kind of grain he was measuring, devised a trick; she rubbed the bottom of the wooden vessel with some fat.

Ali Baba's wife quickly returned home and, after measuring out the gold, carried the measure back to Kassim's wife, not knowing that a gold piece had stuck to the fat at the bottom.

'What have we here?' cried Kassim's wife as soon as her kinswoman had left her. 'So Ali Baba is now too rich to count his gold and has to measure it!'

Jealousy gripped her soul. She sent a servant to fetch her husband from his shop, and told him the story in a fit of rage. 'We cannot let the matter rest at that,' she screamed. 'You must go now and force that wretched brother of yours to reveal to you the source of his riches!'

Instead of being pleased that his brother was no longer a poor man, Kassim, too, was overwhelmed with envy. His heart burning with spite, he immediately went over to Ali Baba's house.

'How is it that you dare to deceive us so?' he cried. 'You go on pretending to be penniless and humble, when you have so much gold that you

cannot even count it. Tell me this moment how
you came by it, or I will denounce you as an
impostor and a thief!'

He showed his brother the gold piece still
smeared with fat, and Ali Baba, seeing at once
how his secret had been discovered, confided to
Kassim the whole story and begged him to keep
quiet about it.

There and then, the greedy Kassim resolved to
take possession of the treasure for himself alone.
He left his brother and quickly returned home,
his head buzzing with a thousand plans.

Early next morning he set out with ten donkeys
to find the cave that Ali Baba had described.
When he came to the rock under the tree, he
stretched out his arms toward it and shouted,
'Open, Sesame!' And exactly as his brother had
told him, the rock opened to let him in. He tied
his donkeys to some trees, entered the cave, then
closed the rock behind him with the magic words.

Kassim was dumbfounded at the sight of the
robbers' treasure, and his very soul was stirred by
the prospect of caravan after caravan carrying the
riches home. He gathered twenty of the largest
sacks of gold and jewels and dragged them to the
entrance. Then he tried to remember the magic
words. 'Open, Barley!' he cried.

But the rock did not open.

The miserable Kassim, preoccupied with the
acquisition of so much gold, had completely forgotten the all-powerful words. Again and again he

shouted, 'Open, Wheat! Open, Barley! Open, Beans!' to the door, which obeyed no sound but 'Open, Sesame!'

And as he stood shaking with rage and terror before the impenetrable rock, the forty thieves came riding up to the cave.

When they saw the ten donkeys tethered near the entrance they leaped down from their horses and scattered around in search of the intruder, brandishing their swords and yelling angry curses. Then the captain pointed toward the rock and pronounced the two words that rent it asunder. The robbers were enraged to find a stranger in their treasure house. They swooped upon Kassim with their swords and hacked him into six pieces, then hung the pieces just inside the cave as a lesson and a warning to other would-be intruders.

When night came and Kassim did not return home, his wife grew very anxious. She went over to Ali Baba's house and begged him to go and look for her husband. Fearing that the worst might have happened, Ali Baba took his three donkeys and rode off at sunrise to the robbers' cave.

With a trembling voice he cried, 'Open, Sesame!' and when the rock opened, he walked in. He was stricken with grief at the sight of Kassim's body cut in pieces. With a heavy heart he took down the pieces and put them carefully together into two empty sacks, which he loaded onto one of his donkeys. He loaded the other two beasts with more sacks of gold, then commanded the rocky door to shut and led his donkeys home.

On reaching the courtyard of his house, he knocked at the door, and it was opened by the slave Marjanah, who was the cleverest and most faithful of his servants.

'Marjanah, my girl,' said Ali Baba, 'today you can give us proof of your ingenuity and wisdom. Your master's brother has been killed by robbers and cut into pieces, but no one must know about it. Think of some way by which we can bury him without arousing any suspicions.'

Then he went to his brother's house and broke the bad news to Kassim's wife.

'Do not grieve, dear sister,' he said. 'Allah has given me more riches than I can use. Come and live in our house, and share everything with us. But no one must know our secret.'

They unloaded the pieces of Kassim's body, and discreetly told the neighbors that he had died suddenly in his sleep.

Then Marjanah went to the shop of an old cobbler in another part of the town where she was quite unknown.

'We want you to do a little sewing,' she said. 'Bring your needles and thread with you. Your work must be secret, and I must blindfold you and lead you to the house.'

At first the old cobbler refused, but when Marjanah slipped a piece of gold into his hand, he allowed himself to be led along the streets and down into the cellar of Ali Baba's house. There she showed him the pieces of Kassim's body, slipped another gold coin into his hand, and bade him sew them together, adding, 'If you work quickly you shall have two more pieces of gold.'

The old man set to work at once and sewed the parts so neatly that no one would see the stitching. She led him back blindfolded to his shop, and returned home to make arrangements for Kassim's funeral. Thus Kassim was buried according to the customary rites, and no one outside the household had the slightest suspicion of the way he had met his death.

When the forty thieves paid their next visit to the cave they were dismayed to find no sign of Kassim's body.

'My men,' the captain said, 'it is clear that someone else knows our secret. We must find out at once who the accomplice of the man we killed is.'

Calling one of the robbers, he said to him, 'Disguise yourself as a holy dervish. Go into the town and find out the identity of the man whose body we cut to pieces.'

Just before sunrise next morning the robber entered the town, and the first shop he saw open was the old cobbler's. He greeted the old man, praised his wares, and engaged him in a friendly conversation.

'I see, good sir, that you begin work before

sunrise,' he began. 'Your eyes must be very good indeed to see so well in the gray light of dawn.'

'Allah be praised, good dervish,' replied the cobbler. 'I can still thread a needle at the first attempt. Why, only yesterday I sewed together the parts of a man's body in a dark cellar without a light.'

'Indeed,' said the robber, 'and who might the man be?'

'That I cannot tell,' the cobbler replied, 'for I was blindfolded and led to the place by an impudent girl, and brought back the same way.'

The robber slipped a gold coin into the cobbler's hand.

'I would like nothing better,' he said, 'than to be taken myself to that house. I will blindfold you, and you can grope your way along the same route you followed yesterday. Take me there and you shall have more gold.'

The cobbler allowed his eyes to be bandaged and, holding on to the robber's sleeve, felt his way slowly to Ali Baba's house; and there he stopped.

'This is most certainly the place,' he cried.

The robber was overjoyed at the discovery. He removed the old man's bandage, slipped a second gold piece into his hand, and sent him back to his shop. Then he took a piece of chalk out of his pocket and with it marked the door of Ali Baba's house. This done, he returned with all possible speed to the forest and told his captain the good news.

When, soon afterward, honest Marjanah went to do the shopping, she noticed the white mark upon the door and thought to herself, 'This is an evil sign, the work of an enemy plotting my master's ruin.'

So she fetched a piece of chalk and made the same mark on the doors of all the houses in the street.

Next morning the thieves came one by one into the town to break into the house their spy had marked for them, and to avenge themselves on everyone who lived in it. But when the robber led them into the street, they were confounded to see that all the doors were marked in the same way, so that it was impossible to tell which was the house they sought. The angry captain sent them back to the forest, with orders to put the foolish spy to death.

'It seems that I shall have to go myself,' said the robber chief.

So next day he rode into the city in disguise and went straight to the old cobbler, who led him to Ali Baba's house. But the captain did not mark the door this time. He gazed long and carefully at it until its very image was engraved upon his memory, and then he returned to the forest.

He called the thieves together and said to them, 'I know the house for certain now. Tomorrow we shall be avenged. All I require you to do is to bring me thirty-nine earthenware jars, each large enough to contain a full-grown man. One of them must be filled with cooking oil, the rest must be empty.'

The thieves, who always obeyed the captain, rode off at once to the market place and returned with thirty-nine large jars. One of these jars they filled with oil, and in each of the others a robber hid himself, on the captain's orders. The chief armed each with a dagger and club, and covered the mouth of each vessel with a muslin cloth, so that the men inside would be hidden and yet breathe freely. Then he loaded his men's horses with the jars, linked the animals together, and drove them toward the city.

When he came to Ali Baba's house, he found the woodcutter seated on his threshold, enjoying the cool evening air.

'Peace be to you, my master,' said the captain with a low bow. 'I am an oil merchant and have been traveling the road these three days. I am a stranger in this city and do not know where to pass the night. I pray that you will give hospitality, for myself and my horses, in the courtyard of your house.'

'You are most welcome, sir,' said Ali Baba kindly.

He took his guest by the hand and led him into his house. Then he ordered Marjanah to help with the unloading of the jars, to feed the horses, and to prepare a hot meal for the stranger.

Now, the captain had told his men that when he threw a pebble into the jars they were to come out of the jars and join him. So they crouched there, patiently waiting for the signal.

Meanwhile, Marjanah, who was busily cooking the dinner in the kitchen, found her lamp going out for lack of oil.

'We surely cannot complain of being short of oil,' she said to herself, 'when there are thirty-nine jars full of it in the courtyard. I will go and take a little from one of them.'

She took her lamp and went to fill it, but as she touched the first jar a voice whispered, 'Is it time?'

The quick-witted Marjanah guessed at once what was afoot, and instead of screaming with fright, whispered back in as deep a voice as she could, 'Not yet!'

As she approached the jars in turn, from each came the same question, and to each she gave the same answer, until she came to the last jar, which she found was in fact filled with oil. After taking what she needed, she returned to the kitchen, lit the lamp, and set to work upon a plan to save her master.

From the last jar she quickly filled a great caldron with oil and set it over the fire to boil. Then she poured the boiling oil into those of the jars in which the thieves were hidden and killed them all.

After dinner the captain of the robbers retired to bed, and at midnight, seeing no light and hearing no sound, he threw his pebble into the yard.

But there was no answer, and not one robber appeared.

'The dogs have gone to sleep,' he muttered.

When he ran down to the courtyard and looked into the jars, he found that all his men were dead. Realizing that his plan was discovered and that he himself might be in danger of his life, he leaped over the courtyard wall and fled. On and on he ran until he reached the treasure cave, where he sat brooding over the calamitous end of his followers.

Next morning, Marjanah took Ali Baba into the courtyard and showed him the jars. He recoiled in horror when he looked into the first and saw a dead man inside, but the girl quickly told him the whole story. Now he rejoiced to hear that all the robbers were dead and was deeply thankful to Marjanah.

'From this moment,' he declared, 'you are no longer a slave, but our own beloved daughter.'

Ali Baba buried the thieves' bodies in a great pit and lived in peace and contentment with his family for many months.

One day, Ali Baba's oldest son, who by now had become a rich merchant with a shop of his own, said to his father, 'I do not know how to repay my neighbor, the merchant Husain, for all the kindness he has shown me since he took the shop next door to mine. I should much like to invite him to our house and give a feast in his honor.'

'Invite him, by all means,' Ali Baba replied. 'He will be most welcome.'

But when the merchant arrived, he said to Ali Baba, 'You do me great honor in inviting me to your house, but alas, I cannot eat with you. I have made a vow never to taste salt or eat any meat flavored with it.'

'That is no difficult matter,' Ali Baba cried. 'I will give orders that no salt be put into our food tonight.' And he hurried into the kitchen to tell Marjanah that she should use no salt in the cooking.

This odd request aroused the girl's suspicions and she looked closely at the guest when she carried the dishes in. Her horror knew no bounds when she recognized the captain of the robbers and saw that he had a dagger hidden in the folds of his robe.

'So that's why the villain would not eat salt with the man he intends to kill,' she thought.

When the meal was over, Marjanah entered the room, and Ali Baba and his son were astonished to see the dress she had put on; it was that of a dancer. Holding a dagger in one hand, she danced gracefully, to the delight of all the company, particularly that of the disguised robber, who took out his purse to throw a gold coin to her. As he bent forward she flung herself upon him and plunged her dagger into his heart.

'What have you done, you foolish girl!' Ali Baba exclaimed, aghast at the deed.

'You have killed the kind old man!' cried the son.

'I have saved your lives!' Marjanah cried. And she showed them the dagger hidden in the visitor's robe, and then told them who he really was and how she had found him out.

When Ali Baba realized that the girl had saved him yet once more, he took her into his arms and said, 'You shall marry my son and become in all truth my daughter; for you have truly earned this reward.'

And so Marjanah was wedded to Ali Baba's son, amid great rejoicing.

For a long time, Ali Baba kept away from the robbers' cave, but when one year had passed he went there with his son and Marjanah. He found the little path that led up to the rock overgrown with long grass, with not a sign of man or beast, and knew that the cave was now perfectly safe. He flung out his arms toward the rock, crying, 'Open, Sesame!' and once again the door opened, revealing the secret treasure untouched since the death of the robbers.

So Ali Baba became the richest and most influential man of his time, and lived in tranquillity and joy until the end of his life.

Epilogue

Night after night, for a thousand and one nights, Shahrazad told King Shahriyar strange and wondrous stories; and so charmed was he by her beauty and gentle wit that at the dawn of each day he put off her execution until the next.

Now, during this time she also bore the King three sons. On the thousand and first night, when she had ended the last of her tales, she rose and kissed the ground before him, saying, 'Great King, for a thousand and one nights I have told you stories of past ages and the legends of ancient kings. May I now make so bold as to beg a favor of Your Majesty?'

The King replied, 'Ask, and it shall be granted.'

Shahrazad called out to the nurses, saying, 'Bring me my children.'

Three little boys were instantly brought in, one walking, one crawling on all fours, and the third held in the arms of his nurse. Shahrazad ranged the little ones before the King and, again kissing the ground before him, said, 'Look upon these three whom God has granted to us. For their sake I implore you to save my life. For if you destroy the mother of these infants, they will find none among women to love them as I would.'

The King kissed his three sons, and his eyes filled with tears as he answered, 'I swear by Allah, Shahrazad, that you were already pardoned before the coming of these children. I loved you because I found you chaste and gentle, wise and eloquent. May God bless you, and bless your father and mother, your ancestors, and all your descendants. O Shahrazad, this thousand and first night is brighter for us than the day!'

Shahrazad rejoiced. She kissed the King's hand and called down blessings upon him.

The people were overjoyed at the news of the King's pardon.

Next morning Shahriyar summoned to his presence the great ones of the city, the chamberlains, the nobles, and the officers of his army. When they had all assembled in the great hall of the palace, he proclaimed his decision to spare the life of his bride. Then he called his vizier, Shahrazad's father, and invested him with a magnificent robe of honor, saying, 'God has raised up your daughter to be the savior of my people. I have found her chaste, wise, and eloquent, and repentance has come to me through her.'

Then the King gave robes of honor to the courtiers and the captains of his army, and ordered the decoration of his capital.

The city was decked and lighted; and in the streets and market squares drums were beaten, trumpets blared, and clarions sounded. The King lavished alms on the poor and the destitute, and all the people feasted at his expense for thirty days and thirty nights.

King Shahriyar reigned over his subjects in all justice, and lived happily with Shahrazad ever after.

ALADDIN AND OTHER TALES
FROM THE ARABIAN NIGHTS
Retold by N. J. Dawood

The ragamuffin Aladdin finds an old lamp which makes his fortune; a prince disappears on a flying horse; a falcon proves wiser than a king . . . These tales of kings and princes, magicians, talking beasts, and shrewd working people, daily entertainment in India, Persia and Arabia over a thousand years ago, are retold especially for children in this vivid, straightforward collection.

THE TALE OF TROY
Roger Lancelyn Green

Freshly and excitingly written, this is the story of Helen and the judgement of Paris; of the gathering of the heroes and the siege of Troy; of Achilles with his vulnerable heel, reared by the Centaur on wild honey and the marrow of lions; of Odysseus, the last of the Heroes, his plan for the Wooden Horse and his many adventures on his long journey home to Greece.